Life

AND OTHER
COMPLICATIONS

HEATHER MULLALY

FAVORED OAK PRESS

Life and Other Complications © 2021 By Heather Mullaly

ISBN: 978-1-7364773-5-9

Book Cover Design & Formatting
by JD&J Design

For

_____

The most authentic thing about us
is our capacity to create, to overcome, to endure,
to transform, to love and to be greater than our suffering.

-Ben Okri

TUESDAY, MAY 10

My friend Caroline Reese lives in a hotel about five miles outside of town. It's a huge Victorian resort called the Ballentine. The first time I saw it, the Ballentine looked like Sleeping Beauty's castle, all covered in vines and thorns. Parts of the roof had caved in, and the interior was scorched. But where everyone else saw a ruin, Caroline's mother saw possibility. She bought the Ballentine and started the slow process of restoring it. Two years ago, the hotel reopened to guests. And this year, the renovations entered their final phase.

Caroline has taken advantage of the last of the construction chaos to commandeer a room in the north wing. She set up her espresso machine and dragged in some comfortable chairs. The space is eventually going to be repainted, so last month I decided to add some color to the walls. I painted bookcases full of leather volumes, curtains to frame the windows, and a ring of quotes about coffee just above the chair rail.

When Caroline's mother saw what I had done to her hotel, I expected her to tell me to paint over it. Which she did. But she also hired me to paint a mural in a room down the hall from Caroline's lair.

The mural room is huge. You can see where a chandelier used to hang and the remnants of crown molding. One wall clearly held a mural at some point. But the paint was so damaged by the fire that I couldn't make out the image. Another wall holds floor to ceiling windows. The last two make up one enormous canvas.

Mrs. Reese wants the whole north wing to house the children's activities, like it did before the fire. So she asked me for a child-friendly mural. Standing there that first day, the images were already taking shape in my mind. Rapunzel's tower would stand in the center, with Hogwarts off in the distance. Peter, from *The Snowy Day,* would need snow-banks to trek through, and Winnie-the-Pooh would want a honey tree.

I've spent the last two weeks planning and prepping the walls. And today after school, I finally got to add the first touches of color to my enormous canvas. I started with the night sky above Big Ben. Once it's dry, I'll be able to add the tiny figures of Peter Pan, Tinkerbell and the Darling siblings flying off towards Never Land.

"You were smart to keep Harry Potter away from Peter Pan and Wendy," Caroline said when she came into the room, her hands full of drinks. "A midair collision would have been unfortunate."

"I thought so."

I climbed down off the ladder, and Caroline handed me

the metal water bottle with "Aly" painted on the side. She kept the mug of espresso for herself.

"Thanks," I said.

She nodded and then closed her eyes, breathing in the scent of the espresso before she took her first, slow sip.

I just watched this ceremony. "Most people drink espresso from small cups."

Caroline opened her eyes. "Most people lack dedication."

I smiled at her.

"Have you decided what to put in the corner?" she asked.

"Not yet."

"What about the gingerbread house from Hansel and Gretel?"

I raised an eyebrow at her. "The witch tries to eat them."

"You don't have to show that part."

"True."

If my foster mother, Mrs. Miller, were telling the story, Hansel and Gretel would have been walking happily through the woods and met a kind old woman who fed them candy without any ulterior motives.

"A gingerbread house would be fun to make."

Caroline's eyes gleamed. "And you could cover the roof with espresso beans."

"You have a problem."

"I have many," Caroline said. "But I am not addicted. Coffee and I are in a committed relationship."

"Does Dylan know about this?"

"Dylan is very open-minded."

"I guess he would have to be, if he's willing to share you with a caffeinated beverage," I said seconds before my phone rang.

It was Mrs. Miller calling in a tight voice. Her tone wasn't that strange. It's the same voice she uses when something has spilled and she's trying to keep up her smile.

I hung up the phone and looked at Caroline. "I have to go."

"What does she want now?"

"I don't know. She just told me to come back to the house."

"But we haven't had time to hide Luke's car yet."

I hugged her. "I'll see you tomorrow."

I left the mural room, ducking under a heavy piece of plastic and maneuvering around work crews to reach the back parking lot. I'm not allowed to drive any of the Millers' cars, and Caroline is grounded from driving for two weeks. Which left our friend Luke as my only way of getting to the hotel with paint supplies. He couldn't drive me himself – he was helping his dad today. But he loaned me his car. So I drove carefully down off Caroline's mountain and into town.

Trinity, New Hampshire is a small town, barely the size of a Boston neighborhood. Instead of high-rises, we're surrounded by mountains and forests and the occasional field of cows. Most of the homes here are old farmhouses with wide porches and steeply pitched rooves. When it snows, Trinity looks like a Christmas card.

I parked Luke's car outside his house and walked the three blocks to the Millers'. A dark blue sedan with Massachusetts plates was parked out front. The car belongs to Mrs. Peters, my social worker. So when I walked into the living room, I was expecting her. It was the man who surprised me. He had graying hair and wore a wrinkled suit.

"Hello, Alyson," Mrs. Peters said. "Do you remember Mr. Raleigh, from the District Attorney's office?"

My body froze. But my thoughts started crashing into each other.

Mr. Raleigh promising me that they were going to put Rick in jail.

Mr. Raleigh asking me questions I didn't want to answer in front of cameras I didn't want to see.

Mr. Raleigh telling me that the case had been dropped. *"I'm sorry, Alyson. We don't have enough evidence to take this to trial."*

My word hadn't been enough.

"Have a seat," Mr. Raleigh said, as if we were standing in his office, instead of my foster parents' living room.

The Millers were sitting tight mouthed on the love seat. There was an empty chair next to Mr. Raleigh and a place on the couch next to Mrs. Peters. I chose the couch.

Mrs. Peters reached over and patted my hand as I sat down.

The Miller girls, Hattie and Gabby, are eight and six, and were nowhere to be seen. They were probably upstairs watching a princess movie. Mrs. Miller is always careful to keep them segregated from the messy parts of my life. I think she would ban messes of every kind if she could.

"Richard Wallace has been arrested, again," Mr. Raleigh said.

I shouldn't have been surprised, not with Mr. Raleigh sitting there in the room with me. But it still took me a few seconds to manage a logical question. "For my case?"

"No. But we're going to need you to testify."

I shook my head. "I don't know anything about another case."

"We know. But we're trying to establish that Richard Wallace's actions toward this girl were part of a pattern of behavior. Your experiences with him can help."

He wanted me to testify. And not just in depositions this time. He wanted me to go to court. To be cross-examined.

Mr. Raleigh leaned toward me. "I know that we're asking a lot. But if we add your testimony to that of other witnesses, we won't have to put the victim on the stand."

He let those words sink in. If I testify, she won't have to.

If the world was fair, I would never have to see Rick ever again. But if the world was fair, this never would have happened to her in the first place.

In the end, Mr. Raleigh didn't have to use the subpoena I saw in his briefcase. I agreed to testify, the way he knew I would. And he gave me a schedule instead. The trial starts on July 5th. My first deposition is a week from Monday.

Across the room, my foster parents had cornered Mrs. Peters.

"We don't have time to take Alyson to Boston for depositions," Mr. Miller said.

"What are we supposed to tell our children?" Mrs. Miller said.

Mrs. Peters' expression was hard as she looked at my foster parents. "When the court gave you permission to take Alyson out of state, one of the conditions was that you would bring her back for all court-required activities. Testifying in a trial certainly meets that criteria." Her eyes moved from one Miller to the other. "As to what to tell your children, I would suggest the truth."

As if that was ever going to happen.

The Millers haven't even told their girls that I have HIV. Mrs. Miller always shoos them out of the room before she watches me take my pills. I don't know how she explains the fact that she won't let me touch anything sharp and makes me wash my hands three times before she lets me help in the kitchen. Maybe they just think I'm clumsy and dirty.

Clumsy I can live with.

Dirty is harder.

Before they left, I asked Mr. Raleigh, "What is the girl's name?"

"I'm sorry, Alyson. I can't tell you the victim's name. We have to protect her privacy."

I understand that. I do. But I also wonder how much our privacy leaves us isolated. This other girl could live next door to me, and I would never know. This isn't something people talk about. But that's what they want from me. They want me to talk about it, to tell the story.

Dear _____,

You don't know me, but I'm going to be testifying in the trial against Rick.

He hurt me too, a long time ago.

I wish I could go back in time and save you from this.

But I can't. The only thing I can do for you is try and help Mr. Raleigh send Rick away for a very long time.

Will you be in the courtroom?

Part of me hopes you won't be there. That you won't have to ever be in a room with Rick again. That you won't have to listen to people talk about you as if you're too broken to ever be put back together.

And part of me wants to see you. To put a face to the fact that I'm not the only one. To know your name.

I hate not having a name for you. It makes it seem like you're not real.

So I'm going to call you Olivia, at least for now.

I don't want to do this, Olivia.

But it's not your fault.

None of it is your fault.

-Aly

WEDNESDAY, MAY 11

Last night I couldn't sleep, because I couldn't stop thinking—about Rick, and the trial, and the girl, and my friends. Luke and Caroline don't know about any of this.

I tried to paint. But after hours of staring at a blank canvas, I gave up, put on running clothes, and left the house while the sky was barely gray.

There was no gradual warm-up to this run. I took off sprinting down the sidewalk. I pushed myself until my legs were asking if I had lost my mind, and my lungs were gasping for air. But it still wasn't enough to distract me. I could still see Rick, still smell his cologne, still hear him whispering in my ear.

The shape came out of nowhere.

One second there was nothing. The next there was a man practically on top of me. I pulled back. Or at least I tried to, but I tripped over my feet and fell, landing hard on the grass.

I was scrambling backwards, my heart trying to explode out of my chest, when a voice said, "Aly?"

I looked up, as he crouched down. Luke.

Luke has grown at least a foot and a half in the nine years that we've been friends. His shoulders are broader, and his face has lost its round edges. But he's still Luke.

I pulled in a ragged breath. "You surprised me."

"You're late, but I surprised you?" he said.

It's Wednesday. We always run on Wednesdays and Saturdays unless one of us is dying. I only felt like I was.

"I'm sorry," I said.

Luke dropped down to sit next to me in the grass. "You didn't do anything."

"Except make you think I'm losing my mind."

Luke smiled. "Well, it isn't the first time."

I love Luke's smile. It's warm and steady and reaches all the way up to his eyes. I love that he has no idea how gorgeous he is when he smiles. I love how much time he spends making other people smile.

My life would be considerably simpler if I loved fewer things about him. Because falling in love with your best friend, who looks at you like you're his sister, is a terrible idea. In my defense, I didn't plan it. It just happened.

"So what's wrong?" he said.

"I didn't sleep much last night."

"Meds or Mrs. Miller's cooking?"

"Both." It wasn't a lie. My drug protocol can cause insomnia and dinner was awful, the way it always is when Mrs. Miller is in a bad mood.

"Someday, they're going to come up with an HIV med that doesn't have side effects," Luke said.

"And Mrs. Miller's cooking?"

"I don't think science can fix that one."

I smiled at him.

Luke stood up and offered me a hand. "Come on. I'll walk you home."

I let him pull me up to my feet. But I didn't want to go home and stand in the shower and think.

"We're running."

"Aly, you're exhausted."

He was right. But I started running anyway. It took him two driveways to catch up.

We've run together for so long that falling into step is almost second nature. I'm typically faster than he is. But today, he was rested, and I wasn't. I had to work to keep up with him. Which was good. I needed the distraction.

When we made it back to the Millers' house, Luke walked up the porch steps with me, the way he always does. But today, he didn't just tell me goodbye and walk away. He stood there, studying me. Usually, I do a pretty good job of covering my emotions. But this morning, I was exhausted, and he knows my face too well.

"You know you can talk to me about anything," Luke said.

And I nodded, wishing so hard that it was true.

THURSDAY, MAY 12

When we first moved to Trinity, Mrs. Miller hadn't planned to tell anyone that I have HIV. But my social worker insisted that she tell my school. Even then, my HIV-positive status was only supposed to be shared with the staff who needed to know. But my third-grade teacher confided in her sister, who told her best friend. Within two days, the whole town knew.

My classmates' parents all said it was fine, that it wouldn't be a problem. But they didn't want their kids sitting next to me in class or playing with me on the playground. Apparently, I looked like the kind of eight-year-old who might bleed spontaneously or start up a brothel in the reading corner.

One whispered secret and I was treated like a leper, while Mrs. Miller was elevated to the status of sainthood.

"You are so good to take her in," the women at church told her.

And Mrs. Miller always said, "We all have to do what we can."

It was one of those church members who suggested that I would benefit from the Children Living with Life Threatening Conditions Support Group at the regional hospital. I didn't want to go. But Mrs. Miller didn't care. She was now playing the part of the devoted parent of a sick child, and sick children belonged in this group.

It didn't turn out that badly. Because on my first day of Group, I met Luke and Caroline.

Caroline's leukemia went into remission two years ago, and she dropped out of Group. (She likes to say that she flunked dying.) But Luke and I are still here, and he drives me out to the hospital every Thursday afternoon after school.

The three of us met in the kids' group. But at age 13, you move up to the Teens Living with Life Threatening Conditions Support Group. The chairs are taller for the teen version and the language is harsher. But otherwise, it's the same. Kids still look like they've been blindsided the first time they come through the door. You don't have to be terminal to end up here, but something has to be working pretty hard to kill you. And you see it in their eyes, that hunted, desperate look.

If they last long enough, the new kids make it through what we call the three stages: crying uncontrollably, breaking things, and finally laughter. I guess that's our version of acceptance, when you can laugh at the thing that's trying to end you.

"Go ahead and take your seats so we can get started," Dr. Klein said this afternoon.

So I sat down in my usual seat in the circle of blue plastic chairs. Luke sat on my right. The seat on my left has been empty since Caroline stopped coming.

"We have a new group member today," Dr. Klein said. "So I want to go over the rules. We have two. What's said in Group, stays in Group. And we tell the truth."

Really, we only have one—we're honest with each other. Or at least that's the ideal.

Dr. Klein looked at the new girl to be sure she understood the guidelines, and then said, "Let's go around the room. Tell us your name, age and diagnosis. Kyle, why don't you start us off?"

He frowned. "Kyle, 16, smurfing osteosarcoma."

The new girl looked confused.

Kyle lost most of his right arm to bone cancer and is still pretty irate about it. When he first came to us, every other word out of his mouth was an F-bomb. Dr. Klein explained that strong emotions were accepted in our group, but not cursing. You have to wait for adult Group for that. She gave him the word Smurf to use for all of his cursing needs. It's a term he now throws down so often, I wonder if he ever slips up and uses it other places.

As much as Kyle complains, he's usually the first one here and the last to leave. In his own way, I think this group matters to him. None of the rest of us have lost an arm. But we're still the closest thing he has to people who understand.

Natalie was next.

"Natalie, 15, leukemia."

Natalie is our tiny resident romantic. She's always been little, but lately she's gotten so thin that her arms look like matchsticks. She won't be the first kid that we lose to cancer. But repetition doesn't make the process any easier.

The next girl said, "Josie, 16, thyroid cancer," and then started crying. Josie has been with us for three months. She cries a lot. We're not sure if it's because of the cancer or because she goes to Saint Margaret's, an all-girls school that could be the inspiration for every mean girl movie ever made.

Dr. Klein nodded to Ben to keep things moving as Natalie put an arm around Josie's shoulders.

"Ben, 17, cystic fibrosis."

Ben has a deep, almost raspy voice. When he first started coming to Group, we called him Batman. Natalie worried that the nickname would hurt his feelings—until he showed up in a t-shirt that said, *Always be yourself. Unless you can be Batman. Then always be Batman.* After that, Natalie relaxed.

The new girl's voice quivered. "Miranda, 14, neuroblastoma. It's a kind of brain cancer."

She looked like she just got hit by a truck. I think those first few times you say the words really are the hardest. Because saying something out loud makes it real.

Dr. Klein nodded to Luke.

"Luke, 18, inoperable brain aneurysm. I call it Larry."

Luke's is by far the most unusual diagnosis in the room. He has a huge inoperable brain aneurysm, a weak spot in one of the major blood vessels in his head. It's been slowly growing for years, stretching out like a balloon. When it bursts, Luke will die. No slow decline. He'll just be gone. It's a reality I don't like to think about.

The circle of faces all shifted to me, and Dr. Klein nodded. I hate this part. Maybe it would be different if I had cancer or a heart defect or something. But I don't. I have HIV, a virus that attacks your immune system. It literally targets the body's defenses. Which is kind of brilliant and kind of wrong all at the same time. Machiavelli would have loved it. Personally, I'm not a fan. Eventually HIV progresses into AIDS. You get sick with something your body can't fight off, and you die. Death used to come fast, but now they have medications that help fight the virus. They can't kill it. But they can buy you time. Enough time to end up in a place like this.

But none of that is why I hate saying the words. I hate saying them, because HIV is a sexually transmitted disease. Sex isn't the only way to get it. But it's the most common, and the one people usually think of first. Which means HIV isn't exactly a comfortable thing to talk about.

But Dr. Klein gave me another look that told me to get on with my introduction.

As I spoke, I didn't look at Miranda. Because I knew that if she's like most people, she wouldn't be able to mask her reaction. I don't blame her. I just didn't want to see her face when I said, "Aly, 17, HIV."

I wasn't looking at her, but clearly my friends were because Kyle said, "Aly's not a slut."

Natalie jumped in. "She got HIV from her mom at birth, and then her mother died when Aly was seven."

"Oh," Miranda said. "That's awful."

I hated the way she was looking at me, with both pity and fear. It was a relief when the conversation moved on.

We finished the introductions, and Dr. Klein opened the floor. She usually lets us steer the conversation and then finds a way to tie it all back to what she calls *purposeful living*. The woman is masterful. She has managed to compare living intentionally to everything from baseball to calculus. Today, the conversation settled on prom. It was a cakewalk.

"It's easy to focus on how things aren't perfect," Dr. Klein said. "How the dress might show a procedure scar, or you don't have the energy to dance to all of the songs. But you can also see prom as a chance to embrace the now."

Agreeing with Dr. Klein is typically the easiest way to get her to move on. So lots of people nodded. I don't know if I didn't nod noticeably enough, or if I hadn't said much today, but Dr. Klein zeroed in on me.

"Aly, are you planning to go to prom?"

Everyone in the room was staring at me. "No."

"Why not?" Dr. Klein said.

Because I'm the girl with HIV.

But I couldn't say that. So I threw out another truth. "I don't have a date."

Luke turned to face me. "I'll take you to prom."

I felt the flush in my cheeks.

Luke could go to prom with anyone, and the whole school knows it. If he took me, it wouldn't just be a pity date. It would be a public pity date. And that is a humiliation that I don't need.

"I don't want to go, but thanks," I said.

Dr. Klein looked disappointed in me but didn't comment.

When we got out to the parking lot, I told Luke, "You should ask Madison."

"She's going with Troy."

That was surprising. "I thought she had better taste."

"So did I."

"You could still ask someone else."

"I know." He unlocked the car. "And I asked you."

"But I don't want to go."

Luke looked at me over the top of the car. "You're sure?"

"Positive."

And finally, he dropped it.

It's not that I'm against proms on general principle. It's that no one thinks of me as someone to date, and everyone knows it. Deadly, uncurable, sexually transmitted diseases are not romantic.

HIV isn't all bad. You can't give blood. So there's no pressure there.

And dating isn't everything. There are lots of other things to do. And you can still have amazing friends.

When Caroline started chemo, Luke and I decided to shave our heads as a sign of solidarity. Luke's parents helped him. Mrs. Miller almost killed me. But either way, if you could have seen Caroline's face the day we showed up in her hospital room bald—she knew we loved her.

Ironically, Caroline didn't lose her hair to chemo. For a while, she was the only one of the three of us who had hair. Then she decided to shave her head in support of us. So we were all bald together. I wish everyone had friends like that. Because I don't know what I would do without mine.

FRIDAY, MAY 13

Today, when Luke picked me up for school, he waited until I had my seatbelt buckled and then handed me a piece of blue construction paper. Written on the small rectangle were the words: *Good for One Favor*, in my handwriting. It was from a pack of coupons I gave Luke as a birthday present when he turned ten. I couldn't believe that he had kept it for all these years, and that I hadn't thought to include expiration dates.

There isn't much I wouldn't do for him, just because he asked. Which meant that he wanted something big.

My face apparently matched my thoughts, because he said, "I'm not asking you to help me move a body."

"What are you asking?"

"I want to take you to prom."

I groaned. "Luke, I don't want a pity date."

"Where does pity come into this?" He backed out of the Millers' driveway. "We hang out all the time. All we're talking about is moving it to a new location with a more formal dress code."

"This isn't a fair use of a coupon."

Luke put the car in drive and looked over at me. "Life isn't fair, Your Highness. Anyone who says differently is selling something."

"And modified *Princess Bride* quotes do not apply to this situation."

"*The Princess Bride* always applies. The question is, are you going to honor your promise?"

That was low, and I told him that. But he didn't look the least bit remorseful.

"This'll be fun," he said.

"I'd rather move a body."

Luke grinned at me. "Maybe next time."

When Caroline got into the car, she didn't seem the least bit surprised that Luke had used an eight-year-old piece of construction paper to get me to go to prom with him.

"He's Luke," she said. "And tonight is Friday, the thirteenth."

"You want to watch horror movies," I said.

Caroline's eyes twinkled. "Yes."

I hate horror movies. But I love Caroline. "I'll ask Mrs. Miller."

"We can run tomorrow afternoon," Luke said.

"You don't want to see us bright and early on a Saturday morning?" Caroline asked him.

"You don't do bright and early," Luke said. "And Aly's going to be in the same building as the mural. I'll be lucky to see her before noon."

"It's like he knows us," Caroline said to me.

Mrs. Miller said yes. So tonight, Caroline and I scrounged for dinner and then ended up in her bed eating ice cream while *Hacksaw House IV* played on mute in the background.

"You don't want to go in there," Caroline said to the three girls who were approaching the ridiculously creepy house.

"You know they aren't going to listen."

"I know. It's as if they have no sense of self-preservation."

The girls went into the house and explored, giving us plenty of time to build up our sense of dread before the shadow of a man wielding an ax appeared on the wall.

I pointed at the ax with my ice cream spoon. "You would think the ax would be a clue that it was time to leave."

"No," Caroline said. "They haven't run yet. They have to run and scream and one of them has to sacrifice herself to try and give the others a chance to escape."

"They could have just not gone into the house in the first place."

"But then there wouldn't be any blood or horrible acting."

"They could have had horrible acting somewhere else."

Caroline shook her head. "It wouldn't be the same."

On the screen, one girl got an ax to the stomach, and I had to look away. "That's disgusting."

Caroline looked from me to the girl whose guts were pouring out of her belly. "Then why are we watching this?"

"Because you like it."

"Aww." Caroline wrapped her arms around me. "You're such a good friend. I would let myself get eviscerated for you."

"Let's hope it doesn't come to that."

"How about *Hacksaw III?* Everyone dies off-screen."

"Sure," I said.

Caroline switched movies, and we started again with three other girls approaching the ridiculously creepy house. The makers of the *Hacksaw* series apparently don't believe in deviating too far from a theme. Shockingly, they haven't won any Oscars yet.

Eventually, Caroline fell asleep. But I lay awake staring at the images on the screen.

I don't know why Luke and Caroline became my friends. I just know that I love them, and I don't want to lose them.

But the trial changes everything. They're going to find out about Rick, and what happened in Boston, and that I lied to them. That I've been lying to them since the day we met.

On the screen, a girl ran silently through the house. There was no escape. She couldn't change what was going to happen. All she could do was postpone the inevitable. But she kept running. Because she couldn't bring herself to let go.

Not yet.

SATURDAY, MAY 14

Early this morning, I left Caroline asleep in her bed and put on my painting clothes: worn-out jeans and an old button-down shirt of Luke's, both splattered with paint. Caroline calls it "Jackson Pollock the Outfit." My painting clothes are practical, but don't really fit with the elegant lobby that Mrs. Reese has worked so hard to recreate. So I used a series of back passageways to reach the mural room on the other side of the hotel without being seen by guests.

When Luke and Caroline and I were growing up, we used to pretend that these passageways were tunnels or sections of a labyrinth. The entire Ballentine was our playground. We transformed one of the tool sheds into a clubhouse and used the surrounding woods as our enchanted forest. The hotel itself played the parts of castle and doomed ocean liner. The glass copula at the very top of the central tower was the crow's nest of our pirate ship. And a portrait on the fourth floor served as a hidden entrance into Narnia.

The only section of the hotel that we didn't go near was the north wing—where the fire started. The north wing was too dark and unstable. And we would never admit it to each other, but we were all afraid of ghosts. Because not all of the children who played in these halls made it out alive.

I used to imagine what this wing was like before the fire. I could picture the girls with huge hairbows and the boys in their knee-length breeches. Through the windows of the mural room, they likely saw the storm gathering in the mountains. They may have even heard the first rumblings of thunder. But I doubt they worried. They were safe inside thick walls. So they went to bed with rain pattering against the windows and woke up to voices screaming, "Fire!"

By morning, the flames were out.

The front of the building looked untouched. There were still flowers in the window boxes. But inside, the hotel had been ravaged. The damage was so extensive that the owners didn't even try to rebuild. They abandoned the place and moved on.

The north wing is where the devastation started, and the north wing is where the renovations will finish, complete with my mural.

I love this project. I love all of the colors. I love imagining children smiling when they see it and getting excited as they pick out the different characters. I love how lost I can get in the process of creating. With a paintbrush in my hand, I can forget the rest of the world exists.

This morning I was so absorbed in my work, that I didn't notice the time until my med alarm started going off.

Usually, Mrs. Miller comes into my room and watches me take my pills, leaning in close enough to be certain that I swallow them. When I stay at Caroline's, Mrs. Reese is entrusted with making sure that I take my meds. But Caroline's mother has a much more relaxed approach. She set an alarm on my phone.

"When the alarm goes off, take your meds," Mrs. Reese said.

This morning, when my med alarm went off, I climbed down off the ladder and was headed back to get my pills, when Caroline came into the room carrying steaming mugs and my pillbox.

I accepted the mug of hot chocolate and pill case with a thank you.

"In your case we support drug use," Caroline said before taking a sip of her beloved.

I had just put my meds in my mouth, when Caroline said, "Who's Olivia?"

I choked and almost spit out my pills. When I had finally gotten them down, I managed the word, "What?"

"I woke up in the middle of the night to go to the bathroom. And your notebook had fallen on the floor."

My heart had risen up in my chest. Every beat was huge. I could feel blood gushing out into my system. The letter to Olivia said too much. And what was on either side of it wasn't any better. How much had Caroline read?

"I didn't read it," Caroline said. "I just saw the name."

For a second, I didn't know if I could believe her. But then I remembered that for all of Caroline's flaws, she doesn't lie. If she had read it, she would have told me.

"Aly?" Caroline said.

I pulled in a breath. "Um, Olivia is what I call my diary." It was true, in a sense.

"You named your diary?"

"It felt strange writing to something that didn't have a name."

Caroline considered that for a second. "If I was going to name my diary, I would pick something more interesting than Olivia."

"Like what?"

"Like Marco the Magnificent."

"Your diary sounds like a self-absorbed circus performer."

I braced myself, waiting for her to ask me what I've been writing about. And the strange thing is, a small part of me wanted her to ask.

But she didn't.

She said, "We're picking Natalie up in an hour."

"Why?"

"We need to find you a prom dress." Caroline help up a hand to stop me before I could get a word out. "Mom and I already talked, and we're paying for it."

"I can't let you do that."

"You don't have a choice. You promised Luke, and it's not like the Millers are going to help you."

It's true. They appreciate the extra stipend that my diagnosis brings them, but they don't actually spend the money on me. The extra money and the martyrdom points are their rewards for taking me in.

"Think of the dress as an early Christmas present," Caroline said.

"It's May."

"A very, early Christmas present."

I knew she wasn't going to let this go, so I finally agreed.

Caroline grinned. "Now, what do you think Luke would like to see you in?"

I frowned at her. "It's not like this is a real date."

"Of course, it's a real date. He's been in love with you forever."

"You're delusional."

"Let's examine the evidence," Caroline said. "He asked you to prom. You turned him down. Did he accept that? No. He took the coupon he had been saving for eight years and cashed it to get you to say yes."

"He was trying to be nice."

But she wasn't listening. "He gets up at ungodly hours to go running with you."

"He likes to run."

"He likes being with you."

"We're friends."

Caroline leaned toward me. "You're more than friends. And you know it."

It's hard enough knowing that nothing is ever going to happen between me and Luke. I don't need Caroline making it worse.

"Can we please change the subject?" I said.

"Fine. But eventually you'll accept that I'm right."

"You think you're right about everything."

"I don't think. I am."

"You were convinced that our middle school principal was demon-possessed."

"Oh, she was," Caroline said. "No one in their right mind would willingly wear plaid polyester."

"Then how do you explain the 1970's?"

"Mass demonic outbreak," she said.

And I laughed.

Caroline wrapped an arm around me and squeezed. "Better."

We picked up Natalie in the next village over. Today she was wearing a t-shirt that read, "The course of true love never did run smooth."

"A Midsummer Night's Dream," I said.

Natalie smiled. "Most people think it's *Romeo and Juliet."*

"Then it would say, 'The course of true love ran off the edge of a cliff."

"True." And then Natalie said something that surprised me. "I hate *Romeo and Juliet.*"

Even Caroline raised an eyebrow.

"Because they both die young?" I asked her.

"Because they both choose to die young. Some of us don't get a choice."

Her words hung in the air until Mrs. Reese said, "Aly, are you looking for a short or long dress?"

When we walked into Betsy's Best Dress, a plump middle-aged woman wearing a nametag that read *Mary Anne* came over to us. "Can I help you ladies?"

"We need a prom dress," Mrs. Reese said.

"Well, most of my stock is already gone," Mary Anne said. "But you're welcome to look at what we have left."

Mary Anne showed us the racks of prom dresses and then left us to browse. Usually, I'm not much of a shopper. But I needed a dress, so I joined the others as they dug through the racks. I quickly decided that most of the dresses were left there for a reason.

"Aly, I want you to find something you love," Mrs. Reese said.

Caroline held out a dress.

"No," Mrs. Reese said.

"Why not?"

"Because she doesn't want to be mistaken for a disco ball," Mrs. Reese told her daughter.

"No," Mrs. Reese said to Caroline's next choice.

"So, it shows a little cleavage," Caroline said.

"We are not putting her in anything she will be afraid of falling out of."

"Do you know your friend at all?" Mrs. Reese asked when Caroline held up her next choice.

"Yes," said Caroline. "And she has nice legs. She should show them off."

"I'm not looking to show anything off," I said. "I just want a dress that—"

"Would be approved by a convent of nuns," Caroline said.

"That doesn't make me self-conscious," I finished for myself.

"You're beautiful," Caroline said. "As long as we don't put you in a horrible dress, you'll be fine."

Mrs. Reese leaned in and dropped her voice. "We do have plenty of options for horrible dresses."

For a while, we tried to outdo each other with awful dresses. Mrs. Reese was holding the top contender, a skin-tight sequined gown with a three-dimensional snake wrapped all the way around it, when I realized that Natalie wasn't with us.

I found her on the other side of the store, standing a foot away from a mannequin that displayed a silk bridal gown. She didn't touch the dress or say a word. But you could feel her longing. Caroline had followed me across the store, and we framed Natalie's small figure.

"That one would swallow you," Caroline said.

I was already looking. I pulled out a dress from the petite collection.

Natalie looked between us, her face confused. "I don't want to try one on."

I held out the dress. "Yes, you do."

Natalie started to protest, but Caroline was already saying, "Mary Anne, we need a dressing room."

Mary Anne frowned. She knew we weren't going to buy a wedding dress with the same certainty that I know that Caroline will start tomorrow with a steaming mug of her beloved.

I could see the word *no* forming on Mary Anne's lips. But Mrs. Reese walked over and said something to the saleswoman. Caroline's mother spoke quietly enough that we couldn't hear her words. But we watched the expression on Mary Anne's face shift. There was deep sympathy in her eyes when she looked back at Natalie. Apparently, Caroline's mother isn't above playing the cancer card when it's needed.

"Of course, we'd be happy to open a room," Mary Anne said, pulling out her keys.

Natalie tried again to protest, but now I had extra leverage. "You don't want to argue with Mrs. Reese, do you?"

And Natalie finally conceded.

Mary Anne not only helped Natalie try on the wedding dress, she brought her shoes and a veil. When they came back out, Natalie was so beautiful it almost hurt to look at her. We all stood and watched her walk slowly over to the three-way mirror.

Caroline pulled out her phone and took dozens of pictures, because this was Natalie, the way her life should have turned out.

In the end, I was the one who found my dress. In a sea of garish colors and clinging curves, it was perfect simplicity. My dress looks like a dancing costume. It's creamy white with inch-wide straps and a scoop neck. The fitted bodice flows out into a full skirt that stops midcalf. It's not something that any of them would have chosen. But I liked it enough to try it on.

When I came out of the dressing room, Caroline said, "I love it," at the same time that Natalie said, "It's perfect."

It was a little disturbing to have them agree on anything.

But Mrs. Reese looked at Mary Anne and said, "We'll take it."

Standing in front of the mirror, I was incredibly grateful, and I told Mrs. Reese that. But I also couldn't shake the feeling that I was pretending as much as Natalie was.

WEDNESDAY, MAY 18

My first deposition is in less than a week. I keep trying to distract myself. But the only thing that can completely consume my thoughts is painting. And I can't paint all the time. My teachers would frown upon that. Today, school provided a distraction—just not a very pleasant one.

Most of the kids at our high school aren't cruel. They just aren't comfortable with HIV. Which means they aren't comfortable with me. They don't know what to say to me or how to act. They don't shun me, exactly. They just give me extra room, an empty seat between us in class, several feet of empty space around me in the hall.

Most of the kids aren't cruel—but there are exceptions. Luke got into the only fight of his life when Brian Dorren said that AIDS stands for Aly Is a Dirty Slut. They were both suspended. Luke still says it was worth it.

No one has made a comment like that since. At least not to my face. But they still show up sometimes in writing. Today, I saw kids clustered around my locker and I knew what I was going to find. But I couldn't bring myself to stand there and read the signs with a crowd gathered around watching like spectators at a car crash.

So I ducked into the bathroom and slipped into the first empty stall, locking the door after me. With my back pressed against the cold wall, I waited until the bell rang. Then I waited another five minutes. By the time I came out of the bathroom, the hallway was empty, except for one figure, Madison Nelson.

Madison was homecoming queen last fall and is a front runner for prom queen. We aren't friends. But today, she was standing in front of my locker pulling down signs. Right next to her head was one that read, *WHORES GET WHAT THEY DESERVE.*

I have one more year of this.

I told myself that I can do anything for a year. Then I can go to art school where there are no lockers.

Madison saw me as she pulled down the last paper. She looked almost as awkward as I felt as she said, "I'm sorry."

I took the signs out of Madison's hands and said, "Thanks," before stuffing them into my bag.

I didn't know what to do at that point but walk away. I passed trash cans, but I couldn't just throw the signs away. Then they would still exist. I don't know why, but when these signs show up, I have this need to hide them, to cover them up. So I walked down the deserted hallways to the art room. Ms. Jones, the art teacher, doesn't have a class last period, so the room was dark. I technically do have a class last period, but I didn't go. I went into the art room and shut the door.

I took Art I with Ms. Jones during the fall semester of my freshman year. I guess she saw something in me. Because every semester since then, she's signed me up for independent study. Basically, that means she keeps me stocked in painting supplies and offers the occasional advice about technique. Last year, when I didn't have the same lunch period as Luke or Caroline, I ate in the art room every day. Ms. Jones never complained. She just let me work or talked to me about painting.

Today, I turned on a few lights, set up a palette, and sat down in front of an easel. When everything was ready, I reached down into my bag and pulled up the first sign my fingers touched. That slightly crumpled piece of paper I set on the easel. It read, *WHO WANTS TO PLAY AIDS ROULETTE?*

At those words, something inside me wanted to curl up so small that I stopped existing. But at least I knew why Madison had been embarrassed.

When Jessie Cooper said that she was going to invite the whole eighth grade to her birthday party, I knew that wouldn't mean me. But then there was an invitation taped on my locker, just like all the others. Everyone was talking about this party. And I was going. I thought maybe, the kids were finally past the HIV. Maybe I could be like everyone else.

Except I didn't know how to be like everyone else. So I asked my friends for help. Luke was fourteen and in high school. He played me all of the popular songs and tried to teach me how to dance—which didn't go well. We eventually agreed that I should stick with the classics: the sway and the jump. Caroline helped me pick out Jessie's gift and figure out what to wear.

By the night of the party, I was as ready as humanly possible and almost excited. Caroline was supposed to be going too, but she got strep. So I was alone walking into the Coopers' basement with my present. Caroline had assured me that Jessie would love the sweater I got her. So I triple-checked that the card was taped to the gift before I put my present with the others. Once that was done, I wasn't sure what to do next. Wishing Jessie happy birthday seemed like a good option. So I walked over to the birthday girl and engaged in one of the shortest conversations of my life.

"Hi, Jessie, happy birthday," I said.

"Oh, hi," Jessie said and then turned back into the tight little knot of girls around her.

"What is she doing here?" someone whispered.

"My mom made me invite her," Jessie whispered back.

And my stupid idea that this was the first of a long line of parties disintegrated. I wanted to leave, but couldn't, unless I was prepared to tell the Millers why I was home so early. Which I wasn't. So I retreated into the far corner of the room and tried to be invisible.

After a while I either developed the superpower of invisibility out of pure will, or the kids lost interest. Because they stopped looking over at me and whispering.

They danced to the songs I knew. And most of them danced as badly as I did. I would have fit right in. If I wasn't me.

When Jessie opened her presents, Caroline was right. She loved the sweater.

"It's so cute," a girl said. "It's too bad it's from her."

Because obviously Jessie couldn't wear it. Not since the whole class knew that I had given it to her.

With the cake eaten and the presents opened, we still had an hour, and nothing to do until Madison threw out the idea of Truth or Dare.

I don't think she would have suggested it if she knew what was going to happen. But either way, there was no going back. Madison was the most popular girl in our class. She wanted to play Truth or Dare, so the other kids all went along with it.

To start things off, Troy Coleman dared Peter Jenkins to lick the toilet. There were no good options for Peter. Either he didn't do it and would be called a coward, or did do it and would be called a toilet-licker. Peter decided to go with the gross factor. He headed for the small half bath in the corner of the basement. The crowd pressed in to watch, shouting with glee and disgust when he actually did it.

Peter was clearly annoyed when he came back to the group.

"Truth or Dare?" he asked Troy.

"Dare," Troy said.

Peter looked around, trying to find something more disgusting than licking a toilet, and he saw me. "I dare you to kiss Aly Bennett for thirty seconds," Peter said, and the toilet was forgotten.

"You're daring me to play AIDS Roulette?" Troy said.

And Peter said, "Yeah."

"You catch HIV, not AIDS," I whispered. But no one heard me. They were all too busy watching Troy.

"I'll do it," Troy said, and the kids all started talking at once.

Troy was big for thirteen and seemed to be growing bigger as he walked across the room. I tried to back up, but there was nowhere to go.

I said, "I don't want to."

But Troy didn't care what I wanted. He grabbed me and pushed me up against the wall, his fingers digging into my arms. I tried to get away, but Troy used his body to pin me to the wall. His mouth was rough and mean as it came down on mine. And then his tongue was forcing its way into my mouth.

Behind Troy, kids were counting off the seconds while his tongue punished me for existing.

When the count hit thirty, Troy pulled back, and said, "God, that's disgusting."

Then he was pushing his way through the crowd to wash his mouth out in the bathroom. Everyone else laughed. Except for Madison. Guilt and pity were competing for top billing on her face. But her pity was as unbearable as their laughter.

I ran, up the basement steps, through the Coopers' house, and all the way back to the Millers'. I could feel the sobs building up in my chest, but I didn't let them out. I pushed it all down. Because if I let myself cry, I wasn't sure that I would ever be able to stop.

Today, there were no tears to hold back, just a tightness in my chest as I painted over the signs one by one, covering the ugly words with huge bursts of color. I created hydrangea blossoms and violets and roses that filled the page. What's buried underneath is irrelevant.

The only thing that matters is what people can see.

Luke and Caroline found me after school. Caroline hugged me so hard it was difficult to breathe. When she let me go, she went off on a tirade about what should happen to the people who had done this. Luke pulled up a stool and sat down in front of me, his eyes focused on mine.

"What do you need?" he said when Caroline paused for breath.

I had been fine. But the concern on his face seemed to bring it all back. Not that I was going to tell him that. He needed something he could fix.

"I can't deal with Mrs. Miller right now."

"Done," he said.

"Rock n' Bowl?" Caroline said.

"Rock n' Bowl," Luke agreed.

"We don't have to," I told them.

But it was too late. Caroline had already pulled out her phone. Seconds later all of our phones dinged. The message had been sent.

The Rock n' Bowl Karaoke Lounge and Bowling Alley is two towns away. But this message is our equivalent to the Bat signal. It's always answered. And by the time we had swung by the Millers to give Luke a chance to convince Mrs. Miller to let me go out on a school night, everyone else was already there.

When we were growing up, the other kids in Group used to call Luke, Caroline and me the Surviving Triad, because we had been around the longest. Ben, Kyle and Natalie are the next circle out. Together, I guess we would be the Surviving Six. Josie and Miranda haven't been around long enough to be invited to the inner sanctum of Rock n' Bowl. But the others were all there.

Inside, we rented the world's ugliest shoes—I'm convinced they make them this hideous so no one will try to walk out with them—and chose our balls—which always elicits a comment from Kyle—before we settled into two lanes.

We come here often enough that you would think we would be decent bowlers. But we're not, except for Caroline. The Ballentine has its own bowling lanes, making bowling one of the few things Caroline can do when she's grounded to the hotel. As evidenced by her bowling skills, Caroline gets grounded a lot. The girl can *bowl*. The rest of us are terrible. Today, Ben struggled to break his personal record of 50. Natalie managed to get gutter balls with the bumpers in. Luke got a strike, in the wrong lane. Kyle threw the ball so hard I'm impressed he didn't leave a dent in the floor. And I dropped my bowling ball on my foot.

The ball smashed into my toes and I had to work to swallow the choice words that wanted to come out of my mouth.

I sank into a chair. "I'm fine."

"Tell that to your face," Caroline said.

"Bowl," I told them.

But Luke headed toward the snack bar, and Caroline started to sit down with me. Only Natalie beat her to it. Nat's face was pale and exhausted. Caroline and I exchanged a glance. She went back to bowling, leaving Natalie to rest in the chair next to me.

"What can I do?" Natalie said.

"You could distract me," I said.

And then regretted that choice when she said, "Have I told you about the fundraiser for Critter Connection?"

By the time Luke came back with a bag of ice, Nat's color was better, and she got up out of her chair. I'm not sure that she should have, but she went back to bowling. And Luke and I didn't try to stop her.

"Shoes this ugly should at least have steel toes," I told him as he sat down in Natalie's vacated chair and picked up my injured foot.

"Dropping bowling balls on your feet isn't part of the game."

He carefully eased off my shoe and sock. A bruise was already starting to form across three of my toes. I winced when Luke touched them.

"Nothing feels broken," he said.

I guess that's a good thing. But I did have the thought that broken bones would have gotten me out of prom.

Luke covered my foot with the bag of ice, and I jumped from the cold. But within a few seconds, I had to admit that it felt better.

"Thanks," I told him.

Luke nodded.

As comfortable as I usually am with him, it felt strange sitting there with my foot in his lap. Strange enough that I started talking. "Natalie is planning a fundraiser for homeless guinea pigs."

"We have a lot of homeless guinea pigs around here?" he said.

"We won't by the time Nat's done."

He smiled at me.

"What kind of fundraiser?" Luke said.

"A *Sound of Music* sing-a-long. And I volunteered you to do 'Edelweiss'. "

He gave me a look.

"They need someone who can sing and play guitar."

Luke shook his head. "Be glad I like you."

"Always."

The lights dimmed, the disco ball started turning, and a pre-recorded voice came over the loudspeaker. "It's time to rock the house!"

The bowlers burst into cheers. The preliminaries were over. It was time for the main event.

I didn't bother with the shoe. I just put my sock back on. Then Luke and I were joining the flow of people as they left their bowling balls and headed toward the back of the building.

The rock half of the Rock n' Bowl consists of a small, carpeted stage. There's a karaoke machine set up on one side. The lyrics show up on a screen at the performers' feet. It's a simple setup, but a ridiculous amount of fun.

A farmer in a plaid shirt and blue baseball cap started us off with "Friends in Low Places." Then Caroline led the crowd in serenading her with "Sweet Caroline."

Like Caroline, I have a standard song: "I Will Survive." I've never liked disco. But I still sing that refrain out like an anthem, because I need the reminder. And tonight, as always, my friends welcomed me off the stage like a hero.

Kyle was slaughtering "Wanted Dead or Alive," when Natalie slipped up beside me.

"Did you ask Luke?" she said.

I nodded. "He said yes."

Natalie beamed. "I knew he would do it if you asked him."

I opened my mouth to tell her that me asking hadn't made any difference. But Natalie got her words out first.

"Luke would do anything for you."

I wanted to ask her what she meant. But Natalie was turning back toward the stage where Luke was stepping up to take the microphone from Kyle.

Luke hadn't said yes because I was the one asking. He was doing it for Natalie. Wasn't he? But then why had he said, "Be glad I like you."

I was confused. And what was happening on the stage didn't make it any easier.

Luke always sings Beatles' songs when we come to Rock n' Bowl. Typically, he sticks with the crowd-pleasers like "Twist & Shout." But tonight, his warm voice sang, "I Will." It was a Beatles' song I didn't know, a song all about love. And what was stranger, was that as he sang, Caroline and Natalie both glanced back at me. I didn't know what to think. Obviously, he wasn't singing to me. He wasn't even looking at me. But as he sang the refrain, even Kyle and Ben were glancing back at me.

Caroline must have said something to the others. She gave them the idea, and now they can't help but read too much into it. It's just a song. A song he wasn't even singing to me. If Luke had feelings for me, he would have said something before now. I literally see him every day. And he's never said a word about thinking of me as anything other than a friend.

Luke was still up on the stage singing. But the people beside me had changed. I wasn't with my friends anymore. I had backed up until I was framed by strangers.

The thought of Luke being in love with me is absurd. I know that. I just wish Caroline would stop talking about it.

MONDAY, MAY 23

Today was my first pre-trial deposition. I told Luke and Caroline that I was going to Boston for a mentoring program. I know that at this point one more lie shouldn't matter. But it does. It weighs on me.

Mrs. Miller drove me to Boston with a tight mouth and a death grip on the steering wheel. I knew that she didn't want me to talk to her. Just like I knew that Mr. Raleigh would.

I wasn't ready to do this. But we were already driving into Boston. Mrs. Miller dropped me off at the justice building and drove away. I don't know where she went or if I even wanted her to come with me. I just knew that I was alone as I went through security and rode the elevator up to the seventh floor.

Mr. Raleigh was waiting when the doors opened.

"Good morning, Alyson," he said. "Your foster mother won't be joining us?"

"No."

"Well, we're going to be right down here."

Mr. Raleigh led the way past cubicles and offices, to a small conference room at the end of the hall. A woman I didn't know was already in the room.

"Alyson, this is Ms. Snyder, your court-appointed advocate," Mr. Raleigh told me.

"Hello, Alyson," Ms. Snyder said.

"Hi."

Ms. Snyder gave me a concerned look. "Have they explained my role?" she said.

I nodded.

Usually, when a minor testifies, they're accompanied by a parent. But if their parents can't be impartial, or they don't have a parent at all, the court assigns an advocate.

"Can we get you all anything?" Mr. Raleigh said. "Water, coffee, soda?"

"Coffee, two sugars," Ms. Snyder said.

"Water, please," I told him.

Mr. Raleigh ducked his head out of the conference room door to pass on our drink orders and then told me, "Have a seat." He pointed to the chair directly in front of the small camera set up on the table.

I sat down. Mr. Raleigh took the chair across the table from me. Ms. Snyder settled into the seat in the corner. Her presence was supposed to be a comfort to me. But all I could think about was that she was one more person who had to hear this story.

There was a light knock on the door. Then a young man brought in Ms. Snyder's coffee and my bottle of water.

"Thank you," I managed.

"Thanks, Tim," Mr. Raleigh said. "Go ahead and close the door behind you."

The sound of the door shutting echoed like a gunshot.

"Just relax," Mr. Raleigh said. "All we're going to do is talk."

I wrapped my hands around the cold plastic bottle of water and worked to pull in a steady breath. There was a window behind me looking into the hall. People passing by could see us, but they couldn't hear us. Only Mr. Raleigh and Ms. Snyder would hear my words. And whoever watched the video.

"Ready?" Mr. Raleigh said.

I wasn't. But I nodded. Because dragging it out for another ten minutes wasn't going to accomplish anything.

Mr. Raleigh hit a button on the camera and then opened his notes. "Please tell us your name and age for the record."

"Alyson Anne Bennett, 17."

"Do you know Mr. Richard Wallace?" Mr. Raleigh said. I nodded.

"Please answer with words," Mr. Raleigh said.

I swallowed. "Yes."

"How old were you when you met Mr. Wallace?"

"Six."

"Do you know the date?"

I shook my head. "No. But I was almost done with kindergarten. So, maybe May."

"And where did you meet Mr. Wallace?"

"At the grocery store."

"Tell me about that," Mr. Raleigh said.

My mother was a cashier at a Shop and Save grocery store. But we never went to her store. She didn't want the people she worked with to know that she used food stamps. She said it wasn't their business. She liked this store better anyway. It was in a nicer part of town.

The night I first saw Rick Wallace, I was supposed to be counting out apples. Mama wanted six, like I was six. I had five when the bag slipped out of my hand and the apples rolled all over the floor. I was scrambling to catch them, when I saw Rick Wallace for the first time. He was a good-looking man in a dark suit and a blue tie.

The other men I knew were mad most of the time. But Rick was different, even in that first moment. He didn't yell at me for dropping the apples or complain about getting his pants dirty. He just knelt down and grabbed a runaway. When we had all the apples back in the bag, he tied the top shut and handed the bag to me with a smile.

"Thank you," I said in my quiet voice.

"You are very welcome." He glanced over at where Mama was looking at melons. "Is that your mom?"

I nodded.

"She's pretty," he said. And then he stood up and walked away.

Mama smiled when I told her that on the way home. She always liked it when men thought she was pretty.

"When did you see him next?" Mr. Raleigh said.

"Maybe two weeks later."

"And where were you?"

"At the grocery store again. But this time, we were in the parking lot."

Mama and I were done with our grocery shopping and were trying to go home. But the car wouldn't start. Mama kept trying to turn it on, but nothing happened. When someone knocked on her window, she jumped. But I didn't. Because it was the nice man in the suit. The one who had helped me with the apples.

Mama rolled down her window and he said, "Do you need some help?"

"I don't know," Mama told him. "It won't do anything."

"Bad battery?"

"It shouldn't be. It's almost new."

"Would you like me to try and jump it for you?" he said.

Mama let out a huge breath. "That would be wonderful."

So he went and got his car and pulled it into the space in front of ours. We watched him take off his suit coat and his tie and roll up his sleeves. With both hoods up, he hooked up the jumper cables. His car purred. But ours didn't make a sound.

He came back to Mama's window. "It's probably a bad alternator." He pulled out his phone and made a call.

"Joe, it's Rick Wallace. I've got a car at the Shop and Save on Second Street. Looks like a bad alternator." He listened and then said, "Thanks, Joe," and hung up the phone.

He leaned down to line his face up with Mama's. "My mechanic will take care of this. But his tow truck is out on another job. Do you want me to call your husband to come get you?"

Mama hesitated. "I'm not married."

She bought wedding magazines and looked at pictures of wedding dresses for hours. But she had never been married. I was a mistake.

"Why don't you take my car," he suggested. "I can wait here for the tow truck."

Mama shook her head. "I couldn't do that."

"You have a little girl who needs to get home to dinner. I'll get your car to the shop and take one of their rentals."

Mama started to say something, but Rick spoke first.

"It isn't very often that I get to play the white knight. Please, let me do this for you." His voice was warm and genuine.

"He's a nice man," I told Mama. "He helped me with the apples."

Mama thought for another second, before she said, "You really wouldn't mind?"

"Not at all." He smiled and reached out his hand. "I'm Rick Wallace."

She shook his hand. "Melissa Bennett."

"It's very nice to meet you, Melissa. And who is the beautiful young lady in the back seat?"

Mama glanced back at me. "My daughter, Alyson."

Rick looked at me and smiled like I mattered. "It's nice to meet you, Alyson. Now let's get you home."

Rick helped us move our groceries into his car and got my booster installed in the back seat.

When Mama and I were both buckled, Rick gave her a card. "Call me tomorrow and we can set up a time to switch the cars back."

"I don't know how to thank you," Mama said.

Rick smiled. "I'm glad I could help. Goodnight, Melissa. Goodnight, Alyson."

We both waved goodnight to him. Then Mama drove us carefully home.

"What happened when you got home?" Mr. Raleigh said.

"We put away the groceries."

I could see our tiny kitchen, with the peeling paint and dark stains on the ceiling. Mrs. Miller would have hated it.

"Mama made me dinner. But she didn't eat. She went on the computer."

After a few minutes, she said, "That nice man who helped us, the one with the black BMW – he's an investment banker."

I didn't know what that meant, but I was glad it made her happy.

I was happy too. Most of the men Mama dated pretended I was invisible. But Rick noticed me. He talked to me. I hoped so hard that he would bring Mama's car back the next day.

"And did Mr. Wallace bring the car back?" Mr. Raleigh said.

"He did."

He brought the car back, just like he promised. And that night, he took Mama out on their very first date. She was so nervous that her high heels kept going *tappity tappity*. But Rick didn't seem to notice. He smiled at her like she was the most beautiful woman in the entire world. Usually, when Mama's dates brought her home, they came all the way back to her bedroom and shut the door. But Rick told her good-night in the hall outside our apartment.

Mama said that she had finally found a good man. And it was all because of me.

TUESDAY, MAY 24

"It's over," Caroline said when she walked into the mural room today.

I was sitting on the ground painting grass around Pooh and Piglet's feet. "What's over?"

Caroline dropped down to sit beside me. "Me, Dylan, this ridiculous attempt at a relationship."

"What did he do?"

Caroline gave me a look of absolute incredulousness. "He mocked Ben & Jerry's."

Which was admittedly a more serious crime than what usually condemned her boyfriends.

"That shows that he has bad taste, not that he's a bad person."

"To my face," she continued as if I hadn't spoken.

"They aren't your relatives."

"They should be."

I painted another strand of grass. "Six weeks. That's a new record for you."

Caroline glared at me.

I lifted my hands in surrender. "I'm just noting. Usually your boyfriends don't make it past the one-month anniversary."

"You're saying I should settle?" Her face dared me to speak such blasphemy.

"You know what I think."

"Well you're wrong. This has nothing to do with my father."

I didn't say anything.

"So things got hard and he left. That's his loss, not ours."

Not a word.

Caroline pointed a finger at me. "And that doesn't mean I think every boyfriend is going to do the same thing. You are reading way too much into this. I just haven't met the right guy."

She has. His name is Garrett. He worked at the hotel last summer. But I've given up trying to point out that he was perfect for her.

I filled my brush with a lighter shade of green. "I guess this means you aren't going to prom."

"Of course I'm going."

I paused, my brush poised in mid-air. "But you don't have a date. And it's in three days."

She shrugged. "I'll find someone or go by myself."

"Or we could stay home and watch *Hacksaw VII.*"

"You are *not* missing prom," Caroline said.

"But you're devastated. You need a girls' night."

"I can be devastated later."

I painted in two more blades of grass. "You can't schedule being devastated."

"Of course I can. We have prom on Friday. Natalie's guinea pig thing on Sunday. I can be devastated Saturday night."

I sighed. It's going to be a long weekend.

FRIDAY, MAY 27

Tonight was prom.

I had half hoped that Mrs. Miller wouldn't let me go. But Luke's dad is the minister of our church, and Mrs. Miller thinks that anything Reverend Harrison approves of must be appropriate. So if Luke could go, there was no reason I couldn't. Besides, this way she would have pictures to show her friends.

Mrs. Miller had failed me. But I didn't stop thinking of possible ways to get out of this. The only sure way would be to pretend to be sick. But if I told Luke I was sick, he would still show up. And Mrs. Miller would find out and start scrubbing everything in sight with Clorox. Which sounded even more miserable than prom. So I let Caroline come over this afternoon to help me with my hair and makeup.

Caroline came through my bedroom door with the words, "I brought The Kit."

It's what she calls the makeup case that is bigger than most tackle boxes. Caroline parked me in a chair in front of my easel and put The Kit down on my supply table.

"Today, you are my canvas," Caroline said.

"Except I would like to be recognizable."

"You'll look like you."

I felt her brushing out my hair and applying make-up. But she didn't let me get up and look at myself in the mirror until she was done.

Caroline had kept her promise. I looked like me. Except there were no dark circles under my eyes or worry lines between my brows. When you paint, the last thing you add are the highlights. And it's those small touches of lighter shades that make the final image come alive. That's what Caroline did for me. She added highlights.

"It's beautiful, thank you," I told her.

"You're beautiful." Caroline said.

She left to get herself ready.

A few minutes before six, I put on my dress. I loved it even more today than I did in the store. And in the privacy of my room, I took the chance to spin. I still can't dance, but the dress swished beautifully.

When the little ones saw me, Gabby said, "You look like a princess."

And Hattie said, "That would make Luke her prince."

They both giggled.

I chose to ignore that idea. Because the last thing I needed was to expect something romantic out of tonight.

But when I got downstairs, and saw Luke in a tux, I was so stunned that I blurted out, "You look like James Bond."

Luke raised an eyebrow. "I do have a pen with a built-in laser pointer."

And I smiled at him.

"You look beautiful," he said.

And the way he looked at me, I thought he might actually mean it.

Mrs. Miller had out the good camera and was taking rapid-fire pictures. The flash was blinding, and we probably looked like deer in the headlights of an oncoming car; but she kept snapping pictures until we were safely out the door.

Luke opened the car's passenger door for me. "Blinded, we're off to a memorable start."

He drove us first to his house, where Reverend and Mrs. Harrison came out smiling.

"Aly, you look beautiful," Mrs. Harrison said.

"Thank you."

"We need pictures," Reverend Harrison said.

"Not until we get the item," Mrs. Harrison told him.

"Should I be afraid?" I whispered to Luke.

"Not unless you've developed a flower phobia," Luke said.

"You got me a corsage?"

Like this is a real date?

Luke gave me a look that wondered if I had suffered a recent blow to the head. "It's prom. What were you expecting?"

"I don't know. I guess that we would go to the dance

long enough to let people see us together and then be home by eight."

"Then you're going to be disappointed," he said.

Luke went into the house and came back with a cold box. Inside it was a wrist corsage made up of creamy white gardenias. It practically screamed of Natalie's influence. I decided to thank her when I saw her at the dance.

Reverend and Mrs. Harrison took their pictures, and then Luke was opening the passenger door for me again.

I've ridden in this car a hundred times. But tonight, felt different. Maybe it was the smell of the flowers, or the feel of the dress, or Luke beside me in a tux. But for a few seconds it all seemed real. And I liked the way it felt.

"Are we picking up Caroline?" I asked him when we pulled up in front of the Ballentine.

"No," Luke said.

The valet opened my door.

"Trust me," Luke said.

And I realized that I did, at least about something like this. So when Luke walked around the car, I took the arm he offered me and we walked into the hotel like a couple out of a film from the 1930's. Inside the lobby, Luke didn't turn toward the restaurant. He led me straight back through the lobby. The doors to the ballroom were open, and I could see the crystal chandeliers twinkling with light. As we came through the doors, there was Caroline and most of the kids from Group, all dressed in formal wear, all smiling at us.

"Welcome to prom," Luke said.

I couldn't decide where to look first, at my friends, all dressed up, or the room, which was gorgeous. The dance floor shone, and the lights twinkled. There was even a large round table set for dinner.

"I can't believe you did this," I said to the group of them.

"We thought you would like this better than the other version," Luke said.

And he was right. But before I could tell him that, Caroline was coming over to hug me.

"This room must cost a fortune," I said as she wrapped her arms around me.

"You're worth it."

I hugged her back. "And your mom didn't make you pay for it."

"That too."

Natalie was a pixie in pink. Ben looked healthy enough that you might not guess that cystic fibrosis is slowly smothering him to death. Josie and Kyle were both smiling, at the same time. The new girl, Miranda, wasn't there. I thought she might have gone to the official prom. Or as I was thinking of it, the gaudy knock-off.

Caroline yelled, "Let's get this party started!"

Natalie's neighbor, Graham, hit a button, and the opening bars to "Footloose" started up. I laughed.

"We can't have an unofficial dance without the official anthem of unofficial dances," Luke said.

"Of course not," I told him.

And then Caroline was grabbing my hand.

What followed could only be described as loosely coordinated mayhem. And it was fabulous. The music included songs that have never been grouped together in the history of humanity. But I loved it. Because it meant that each one of them had added to the list. The classic rock was Luke. And the heavy metal was Kyle. Josie added country, and Ben threw in some R&B. Caroline's were the bands no one else had ever heard of. And when the music slid into "Unforgettable," it had to be Natalie's.

Nat King Cole's deep rich voice seeped into the room, and I smiled, until I realized that all of the others were pairing off.

In less than a minute, Luke and I were the only ones left. He offered me a hand.

"I've never done this kind of dancing before," I said.

"That's okay," he said. "I have."

I put my hand in his, and Luke led me a little way onto the dance floor.

"Where did you learn to do this?" I asked him.

"I go to a lot of weddings." He turned to face me. "Do you know where your hands go?"

I nodded. "I do watch old movies." I put my left hand on his shoulder, feeling the smooth fabric of his tux jacket under my fingers.

I knew what was coming, and I tried not to flinch when his right hand came to rest against my lower back. But my muscles still tensed up at his touch.

"Try to relax." Luke took my right hand in his left, and we started to dance.

I did try. I wanted to be smooth and graceful. But I kept stumbling.

"Aly."

I looked up.

"Try looking at me instead of the floor."

"I don't want to step on your toes or fall on my face."

"My toes are tougher than they look," he said. "And you're not going to fall. I've got you."

It's what you say to people who are dangling over the edge of a cliff.

"Just look at me," he said.

So I looked up at him. My whole body was tight. But Luke's voice was steady and calm. "You don't need to try and guess what I'm going to do next. You can feel it."

At first that didn't make any sense. But after a few steps I began to understand what he meant. I could feel how his right hand pressed gently into my back when he was drawing me toward him and how his left arm tightened when he was asking me to take a step backwards.

Barely a breath separated us. But I didn't feel trapped. And for a few minutes, I could pretend that we weren't ourselves. That Luke wasn't terminal, and I didn't have HIV. Instead, we were newlyweds dancing together at our wedding. It was easy to imagine. We were already in a ballroom, surrounded by our friends. Luke had the tux, and I had a white dress that just needed to extend to the floor and add a few flourishes. We were on the edge of everything good.

Until the song ended. The carriage turned back into a pumpkin. We became ourselves again. And Luke let go of my hand.

"Thanks for the dance."

"Anytime," he said, just before he walked away.

I stood alone on the dance floor, overly aware of the empty space that surrounded me. Luke had danced with me because it was polite. But he hadn't stayed.

I forced myself to push that thought away and join the others.

After dinner, we all ended up on the back lawn, stretched out on blankets Caroline had dug out of a linen closet. The hotel was a blur of soft lights in the distance. But the space surrounding us was nothing but inky black sky and stars. Millions and millions of stars.

"The stars are a nice touch," I told Luke.

"They're part of the deluxe prom package," he said from the darkness beside me. "The basic package only comes with twinkly lights."

I leaned back onto my hands and stared up at the beauty of our personal planetarium. "There are so many I can't even find the North Star."

The dark shape of Luke's arm pointed to my right. "There."

I followed the line of his sleeve and twinkling at the end was Polaris.

"So that's the Little Dipper." I traced back from the North Star. "And the Big Dipper."

"I see Orion," Luke said, "and Genghis Khan."

"We're making up constellations now?"

"Why not?"

"Okay." I looked back at the millions of tiny lights spread across the sky. "I have an artist's palette and Mickey Mouse." I used a finger to connect the dots for him.

We sat there in the dark pointing out constellations until my arms were so cold I started to shiver. I felt more than saw Luke take off his tuxedo jacket and wrap it around my shoulders. I slid my arms into the sleeves, feeling the jacket's warmth against my cold skin.

"Thanks," I told him.

"Sure."

"I mean for more than the jacket. The whole night. I was dreading prom."

"I kind of figured," he said.

"But tonight has been amazing."

"Good. You deserve an amazing night."

Luke's white shirt glowed a little in the dark. And I re-alized that he was closer than I thought. But that realization didn't startle me. I liked knowing he was there, inches from me. It was the way we were on the dance floor, before the song ended, and he walked away. But this time he didn't pull away. If anything, it felt like he was moving towards me.

I knew that wasn't possible. There was no logical reason why he would do that. I was sure that I was imagining it—until his arm brushed against mine.

Then my heart started beating so fast I felt dizzy.

Luke was close enough that I could hear his breaths.

But he didn't close the rest of the distance. He paused, waiting. And in that second, I felt another rush of love. Because Luke wasn't going to push me into anything; he was giving me a choice. And for once, I knew what I wanted. I leaned toward him, shortening the distance between my cold lips and his warm mouth. Luke's breath brushed against my cheek. Excitement was tingling through my body. He was going to kiss me. His body heat was warming up the air around me.

And then it was gone.

Luke had pulled back.

And where I thought there had been warmth, there was nothing but cold, empty air.

For the span of a breath, I was stunned and confused. Then the excitement in my chest twisted into something sharp and throbbing.

What's wrong with me?

Why would I think Luke was about to kiss *me*?

None of this was real. He asked me to prom out of pity. Just like last year he asked Becky Sylva, who has Down Syndrome.

But for some stupid reason, I thought he had actually wanted me.

I could see Luke's white shirt in the dark, at least well enough to know where he was. Which meant he might have seen my white dress. He could have seen me leaning in with my eyes closed like one of the ugly stepsisters in a bad rendition of Cinderella.

Humiliation burned the cold out of my face, and self-loathing sprouted up in the wake of the heat. I'm repulsive. Filthy. And stupid. So incredibly stupid.

"Aly?" Luke's voice said through the dark. "Are you okay?"

No. But I wasn't going to say that word out loud and make the moment any worse.

"It's getting late," I managed. "Can you take me home?"
"Oh. Sure."

Luke drove me home. But for once, we didn't talk. We sat in awkward silence.

I wished so badly that I could think about anything else, but I was caught in a humiliation hangover and nothing would penetrate my thoughts but that one horrible scene playing over and over again. Me leaning in, Luke pulling back. He practically jumped he was in such a rush to get away from me. I kept my hot face turned toward the passenger window and willed the car to move faster.

When Luke pulled up in front of the Millers' house, he barely had time to put the car in park before I was pulling off my seatbelt and opening the door. I threw a garbled thank you at him and rushed to get to the front door before he got out of the car. But I shouldn't have worried. For the first time in his life, Luke didn't walk me to the porch. He waited long enough to see me open the front door, and then he drove away.

He was in that much of a rush to get away from me.

SATURDAY, MAY 28

I told myself it wouldn't hurt so much in the morning.
I was wrong.

SUNDAY, MAY 29

I didn't go running yesterday. It was Saturday. But I couldn't face Luke. And for once, he didn't show up at the Millers' to find out what was wrong. It was better that way. I didn't want to see him. But at the same time, I hated that he didn't show up. Because it means that everything's changed.

I didn't want to see Luke. But tonight was the *Sound of Music s*ing-a-long that I had convinced him to join. I didn't want to go. But I had promised Natalie. And I knew I had to see Luke eventually. At least this way it would be with a crowd.

When Caroline picked me up for the event, I didn't tell her what happened Friday night. The whole situation was humiliating enough without having to relive it. So I got into her car and said nothing about Luke. I wasn't sure what we were going to talk about, but I shouldn't have worried. Caroline skipped over her scheduled devastation and filled the entire trip with commentary about prom. I didn't hear most of it.

But when we got to Redford Village Hall, I couldn't ignore the six-foot-tall guinea pig cutouts that flanked the front doors of the building.

"Holy guinea pigs," Caroline said.

All I could manage was, "Wow."

Caroline leaned toward me. "They're following me with their eyes."

I pulled open the door. "Don't look back."

Inside, we found a distraught looking Natalie waiting for us.

"What's wrong?" Caroline and I said at almost exactly the same time.

Natalie led us away from the people who were beginning to arrive. When we were clear of the crowd, she whispered, "One of the clients is missing."

"Clients?" I asked.

"The guinea pigs we help. Houdini was in the habitat by the doors into the hall, and now he's gone."

"You named a guinea pig after an escape artist?" Caroline said. "Who does that?"

"Not helping," I mumbled.

"You might as well name the thing Roadkill."

I shot Caroline a look before I told Natalie, "We'll find him. Why don't you start with the auditorium? Caroline can look backstage. I'll do the lobby."

So, we split up to look for a missing rodent at a movie sing-a-long. I've had stranger days.

I searched every inch of the lobby, trying to look casual

as I ducked under tables and crawled into corners. Arriving guests gave me strange looks, but I ignored them.

I unfortunately couldn't ignore Luke when I stood up and almost ran into him.

He took a step back. Luke, who always seems so sure of himself, looked awkward as he said, "Hi."

I couldn't look him in the eyes. "Hi."

For a few seconds, we said nothing.

Luke looked from his guitar case to my face. His fingers tightened on the case handle. "I'm sorry."

I was working to sound casual, but my words still came out forced. "Sorry for what?"

For being stupid enough to invite me to the prom in the first place?

"For leaving so fast Friday night."

"Oh. I didn't even notice."

It was a lie. But I couldn't tell Luke Harrison that I had leaned against a wall in the Millers' foyer and struggled not to cry.

Luke was studying my face, trying to see past the mask I was fighting to hold. I guess I won because he said, "Are we okay?"

"We're fine."

We're right back where we started. He's still Luke. And I'm still the girl with HIV.

"Good," he said, and seemed to mean it.

It didn't feel good to me. But I guess we were at least talking to each other.

"Interesting shirt." I pointed at the *I ♥ Guinea Pigs* t-shirt he was wearing.

"Natalie made them for all of the musicians."

Caroline came back into the lobby holding a metal trash can.

"I found Houdini. And he bit me." Caroline glowered down into the container.

I said, "You did make fun of his name and stick him in a trash can."

Neither of those observations improved her expression.

"Did his teeth break the skin?" Luke asked.

"No."

That was something, at least. Caroline hates hospitals, and I didn't want to have to drag her to the ER to get her treated for an infected rodent bite.

"They want all the musicians backstage," Caroline told Luke.

"Okay. I'll see you guys after," he said.

I didn't watch him walk away. Instead, I watched Caroline put the stray guinea pig back in his cage and close the latch. Houdini chattered at her angrily and then waddled into a wooden house.

When the program started and Caroline and I slipped into the back row of the auditorium, I avoided looking at Luke. But when it was time for "Edelweiss", he walked out to the front of the stage with his guitar in his hand, and I couldn't stop looking at him. Only Luke Harrison could make an *I ♥ Guinea Pigs* t-shirt look that good. I watched him slip his guitar strap over his head and take a second to tune the instrument before he began to play. I was half dreading the moment when Luke started to sing. But my dread has never kept things from happening. And tonight, was no exception. His warm, steady voice still filled up the hall, and I could do nothing to keep that warmth from sinking into me.

Luke has always been upfront with me, about everything. We're friends, nothing more. And that should be enough. But there was an ache in my chest anyway. Because I want there to be more.

I want exactly what I can't have. Because I'm the girl with HIV.

Dear Olivia,

Have they told you about HIV yet?

They know that Rick is HIV-positive. So I'm sure they've run the test. But they may not have told you if your test came back positive. They didn't tell me right away. They thought I had too many other things to cope with. So that news came later, an undetonated grenade left over from a war that was supposed to have ended.

Every two months I have to go to the hospital and have labs drawn to see how well the HIV meds are working. When they pull up my file in the lab, there's a flashing warning that reads *HIV-Positive*. It's the human equivalent of having a *Biting Risk* sticker on a dog's file at the vet. At least in my case it just means that the phlebotomist should wear double gloves, not fit me with a muzzle.

The day after the blood draw, I go to see my doctor and hear the results.

The pediatric waiting room is segregated into two sections: sick and well. Apparently, I don't fit neatly into either category. Because they always take me straight back to an exam room. The nurse takes my vitals, asks Mrs. Miller if she has any questions, and then leaves me with a pamphlet about living with HIV.

I am the clinic's only pediatric HIV patient, so for the first four years that we lived here, I got to have the same pamphlet every time I came in. On the front of the pamphlet was a cartoon of a thuggish-looking blob labeled HIV beating up a poor defenseless white blood cell until a pill came to save the day. The pill even had a cape.

When I turned thirteen, I got to move up to the teen version. This pamphlet doesn't have a cartoon. Instead it has a slogan on the front: *You Can Still Be Cool with HIV.* Because apparently my coolness was in question. I have read this pamphlet so many times I have it memorized. So, I use the paper to make origami flowers. So far, I can make tulips, and roses, and I'm working on daffodils.

The bi-monthly blood tests look at two things. My viral load, and my CD4 count—which indicates how healthy my immune system is. The last time I was in, my CD4 count was normal. But my viral load had doubled.

"This happens," Dr. Jordan told me. "I'll talk to the team at Dartmouth about adjusting your medications."

If you do have HIV, they'll tell you that with the right medications, you can potentially live for decades and have an almost normal life. The medical community is proud of their miracle drugs, and they should be.

What they don't understand is that those miracle pills come at a cost. Because every time you take one, you're reminded of Rick.

The same pills that give you a future, mean you can't get away from the past. Rick stays right there with you, reminding you every day, that you're dirty and broken. That he ruined you.

If he gave you HIV there is nothing I can do to undo that. I can't make it so that this didn't happen. I can't give you back the life you had before Rick. I can't make you whole again.

Mr. Raleigh says that my testimony will help you. But the truth is I can't do anything about the things that really matter. And I hate that. I hate it so much.

-Aly

MONDAY, MAY 30

Today was Memorial Day. My friends went to a cook-out at Luke's. But I had to go to Boston and walk through an almost deserted building to the conference room I've started to hate.

This time, I had barely sat down when Mr. Raleigh asked his first question.

"How long had your mother and Mr. Wallace been dating when he invited you to move into his house?"

"A few weeks," I said. "Maybe a month. It wasn't long."

I could hear Mama's voice in my head. "I know it's fast. But Rick loves us so much. He wants to be a family."

I had never been part of a family. My birth father left before I was born. It had always been just Mama and me. But the way she said the word *family* I knew it was something good.

"How did you feel about moving in with Mr. Wallace?" Mr. Raleigh said.

I wanted to tell him that I knew it was a terrible idea, that my mother had dragged me along. But I told him the truth. "I was excited."

I liked Rick and his house. It was so much nicer than our apartment. Bigger. Cleaner. Quieter. Rick's was the kind of place where you would never wake up to screaming voices in the middle of the night or come home to police cars parked out front. Rick's house felt safe.

The day we moved in, Mama couldn't stop talking. She loved everything, the good neighborhood, the granite countertops in the kitchen. Even the furniture was perfect.

I liked the house too, but most of all I loved my room. It was painted a pale yellow and had a big canopy bed, like something a princess would sleep in. There was a dollhouse and a bookshelf full of books. I thought Rick must have bought the things for my room from Goodwill. Because every book in my bookshelf had a name written in it: Jenny, or Becca, or Katie.

Mama was a little nervous about the swimming pool in the backyard, because I didn't know how to swim. But Rick promised to teach me. Mama's boyfriends had promised things before. But Rick actually kept his promise. He took me to the store that first day and bought me a bathing suit, a bikini with ruffles. Mama said it was adorable. And that afternoon, while Mama unpacked, Rick gave me my first swimming lesson.

Rick taught me to float on my back. At first, he supported me in the water, his left hand on my back, his right hand under the backs of my thighs. When I could float without help, Rick cheered and blew a raspberry on my stomach. The funny sensation made me laugh and wiggle. Rick scooped me out of the water to blow a line of raspberries down my bare stomach that made me laugh even harder.

I was so happy. But when I went back to my room to get dry clothes, I found Mama there unpacking. And her face was worried.

"What's wrong?" I asked her.

"They've already rented our apartment. If this doesn't work out, we don't have anywhere else to go."

I hadn't known I was supposed to worry about it not working out.

Mama looked at my face and adjusted hers. "I'm being silly," she said. "As long as Rick loves us, everything will be fine."

So I didn't worry. Because Rick told us every day that he loved us. And more than that, he showed us.

One night during our first week at Rick's house, I woke up crying from a bad dream. I went looking for Mama, but I couldn't find her in that big house. I was panicking by the time Rick found me.

He picked me up and squeezed me. "It's okay," he said. "Nothing is going to hurt you here."

I buried my face in his shoulder and held on as he carried me back to my room. Rick tucked me in and then sat beside my bed until I fell back to sleep, just like a real daddy.

I wanted a daddy so much. To be like other kids. To have someone to push me on the swings and to protect me from monsters and big dogs. One time, I saw a man run right in front of a car to save his little boy. I wanted someone to love me that much. And finally, I had found him.

Mama was happy too. She didn't have to work at the Shop and Save anymore. Rick said that taking care of me was the most important job in the world. He didn't even expect her to clean the house. He had a cleaning lady, named Catalina, who did that. All he asked was that Mama made dinner and cleaned up afterwards. So while Mama made dinner, Rick gave me my bath.

I loved Rick and I wanted him to love me. But sometimes, it felt strange having a daddy. Where Mama had rushed through drying me off after my bath, Rick took his time. He dried me slowly with one big towel, and then went back with a second towel and did it again. I wasn't allowed to wear pajamas or underwear at night anymore, only nightgowns. Rick said that my skin needed time to breathe. At first it felt strange having the air slide up my bare legs. But Rick and Mama said I looked so beautiful. And after a few days I got used to it. It was just one more thing that made this new life different from our old one.

After dinner, Mama would do the dishes while Rick took me into the living room to watch a movie. He always sat me in his lap. And the house was always so cold that he put a blanket over us.

At first it was nice. I liked being cuddled up close with his arms around me. It made me feel special. Like I really was his little girl. I didn't even notice that his right hand was on my leg, first over the blanket, then under the blanket.

I didn't like it when he nudged my knees apart. But Mama had told me to be good. And good girls did what they're told. So, I watched the TV and pretended not to notice that his hand was inching its way up the inside of my leg.

One night, his hand made it all the way up to the top of my thigh. I froze. I didn't know what he was doing. I just knew that it felt wrong. And I wanted him to stop.

But I didn't know how to say that without making him mad.

Rick was everything Mama had ever wanted. He was generous and kind. He loved us. And I loved him. But if I made Rick mad, it could all go away.

"Did you tell Mr. Wallace to stop?" Mr. Raleigh said.

And I had to work to swallow the rock in my throat.

"No," I whispered.

"Did you tell anyone that he was touching you?" Mr. Raleigh said. "Your mother, a teacher?"

"We can't ruin this," Mama had told me. "We won't ever have another chance like this."

To be loved. To be a family.

"I didn't say anything."

If I had handled it differently, maybe it would have ended there. If I had known what to say— but I didn't. I just learned to watch TV and pretend not to notice what was happening under the blanket.

Dear Olivia,

I keep picturing you sitting on Rick's lap in the living room.

Is that how it started with you?

Did he ease you into it?

Moving so slowly that you couldn't even tell when it went from good to bad?

Was it like he was drawing you a bath?

At first the water felt nice, relaxing.

Then the temperature rose a little.

Then a little more.

Until it was hotter than you liked.

But you adjusted.

It became your new normal.

And the temperature kept creeping upwards.

Degree by degree.

Until he was boiling you alive.

-Aly

WEDNESDAY, JUNE 1

I've been painting, a lot. Because when I paint, I can push everything else away. The problem is, I'm spending so much time working on the mural, I'm going to finish it before we ever get to the trial. I have to find more to do. I've considered painting over a whole section and starting again. But before I did anything that drastic, I decided to look for anywhere I could expand. Which brought me to the blackened wall that holds the original mural. Mrs. Reese is planning on having it torn out and the wall rebuilt. But I wondered if any of the old painting could be saved.

There was no way to know without cleaning it off. So I got a bucket and a sponge and began the delicate work of trying to remove the soot without damaging the painting underneath. Parts of the wall are damaged beyond saving. But there's a section, right in the middle, that looked like it might be intact. So I started the slow and careful process of trying to clean away the ash and the grime. What I found underneath was the image of a little girl in a white dress.

She was alone. Whoever had surrounded her in the original mural was gone. But her face was happy. The artist had created something beautiful. Something pure and innocent. Something the fire had ravaged.

Whole sections of the girl's face are smeared with greasy ash. Her dress is blackened. Pieces of her portrait crumbled when I touched them. She's ruined.

I left the blackened wall the way it was. I hope Mrs. Reese does tear it out and start again. Because I don't want to look at that girl. I don't want to think about what happened to her. I don't want to remember everything she lost. I don't want to touch her and watch her fall apart.

I went back to the side of the room where I was supposed to be and grabbed an oversized brush. In seconds I ruined a section of mural that had taken me days to paint. I was still holding the brush, looking at what I had done, when Luke walked into the room.

I was so distracted trying to figure out how I was going to explain this, that I didn't really see his face. But then he said my name. And with the tone of that one word, I knew that something was wrong. Something much bigger than the awkwardness we've been living with since prom.

His head.

Or Caroline had relapsed.

Or the lie.

He found out that I've been lying to him since the beginning, that I lied to him about my visits to Boston. He found out about Rick—

Luke's voice was hollow. "Josh Collins is dead."

I stared at Luke, trying to make sense of his words.

Josh Collins isn't terminal. He's just a regular kid who goes to our high school. He used to sit two rows ahead of me in English.

"Car accident," Luke said.

I could barely process the words. Josh Collins. Dead.

I must have looked as stunned as I felt, because Luke walked over and opened his arms. I pressed myself into his chest, feeling his shirt against my cheek, his arms wrapping around me, and wished that he never had to let go.

FRIDAY, JUNE 3

My mother never took me to church. She said that churches didn't want people like us. She had grown up going to church. And she went every week until she was sixteen and her stomach swelled so much that people started whispering. After that, she never went back.

The first time I went to church with the Millers, I saw the people looking at me and I was sure that they could see past my clothes, see every terrible thing I had ever done that wouldn't wash away. I wanted to run and never come back. But the Millers made me go every Sunday. And in our cluster of small towns, funerals are always held in churches. So today, I had to go to church for the second time this week. Because today was Josh Collins' funeral.

My friends and I go to a lot of funerals. It's one of the downsides of Group. But today's service was different. Josh Collins hadn't even been sick. And the congregation was more stunned than resigned. They hadn't expected this one.

The six of us go to so many funerals that we have an ongoing bet about the music. Two years ago, we each chose a hymn. Every time our hymn is played at a funeral, we get a point. So far, I'm winning, by a lot. And today another point was added to my tally when the organ started into a strangled rendition of "Amazing Grace." Kyle says that he was going to pick "Amazing Grace," but I beat him to it. Life isn't fair.

I don't like "Amazing Grace." I've heard it played at too many funerals. And watched too many caskets rolled down the aisle to its tune.

We don't carry caskets in the valley anymore. Not since the members of the VFW dropped a coffin in the middle of the Trinity Baptist Church. The box opened and eighty-six-year old Roger Nelson rolled out onto the church floor, landing at the feet of Kelly Durgan. As the pall bearers tried to get him back into his box, the nearby mourners all saw that the corpse had a huge grin on his face. The family told anyone who would listen that Roger was always smiling, and it had nothing to do with getting a look up Kelly Durgan's skirt. But after that, caskets were rolled, not carried.

There is no talk of long lives well lived at the funerals I attend. The discussion centers on a young life cut too short and what a wonder the deceased was. According to the speeches made at funerals, all terminal kids are selfless angels, who never feel sorry for themselves and face death without fear. Which is ridiculous. Some terminal kids are nice, some aren't. All of us feel sorry for ourselves at some point. And we're terrified of dying. We just get over it. Because we don't have another choice. There are too many things in our lives that we can't control.

What Josh couldn't control was the truck that hit his car at 60 miles an hour. The police decided that the accident was Josh's fault. At this point, I don't think it matters. Either way, he's dead.

Caroline sat beside me on the pew. I was probably the only one who could see the strain around her eyes. Josh's death was hitting her as hard as the kids who've gone into remission, only to have a resurge of cancer end them. She doesn't want to think about this happening to her. Caroline prefers to be invincible.

Two rows ahead of us, Madison Nelson was crying. Josh was her cousin. They grew up together. Madison isn't like us. She hasn't built up a shell against this kind of loss. She was devastated, and the rest of the family was so caught up in their own grief that they didn't notice. It was Luke who slipped out of our row to go put an arm around her. She cried on his shoulder for the rest of the service.

It shouldn't have bothered me. Madison needed someone. And Luke is good at this. He was the natural choice. But I still wished it wasn't him. Because it hurt to see them together. Even though they're perfect for each other.

Maybe because they're perfect for each other.

Caroline has her own post-funeral ritual. The rest of us always meet up at Luke's house. If it was anywhere else, the Millers wouldn't let me go. But they can't call a gathering at the minister's house inappropriate, even if we all spend the night. Instead, Mrs. Miller always threatens me within an inch of my life if I embarrass her. As far as I know, I haven't yet.

Luke's parents know that there aren't words to make us feel better. And they don't try. They always hug us and then go upstairs, leaving us with lots of food and each other.

Our post-funeral menu is always the same: hot dogs and Oreos. Luke, Caroline and I knew a girl in Kids' Group named Morgan. She had a brain tumor and a mother who was convinced that a clean diet and all natural everything would make it go away. It didn't work. The cancer got worse.

Luke's mom took Luke, Caroline and me to see Morgan in the hospital. We were nine and ten and not sure what to say. But Morgan talked to us about all the things she wished she could do, including eating hot dogs and Oreos. We couldn't find hot dogs in the hospital. But we did find a vending machine that sold packs of Oreos. Luke raided his mom's purse, and we bought every pack the machine had. Eleven packs times six cookies per pack meant sixty-six Oreos and proof that my teacher wasn't lying when she said our multiplication facts would be useful. Morgan's eyes widened as I broke open the first package of contraband, and we ate Oreos until her mother caught us.

Morgan died a few days later. After the funeral, Caroline and I went back to Luke's house, and we ate hot dogs and Oreos until we all felt sick. Mrs. Harrison doesn't like to have cookies in the house. But this became her exception—Double Stuf Oreos after funerals. Because if we're going to eat Oreos, we might as well go all in.

Tonight, we were mostly done with our post-funeral meal, when Ben said, "I'm starting up Mount Washington after school gets out."

Ben can barely walk from one side of our school to the other without struggling for breath.

"Is that safe?" Natalie said.

"I'm dying," Ben said. "Life isn't safe."

And a heavy silence fell over the room. No one said something inane like, "You'll be fine." Ben has an incurable disease that is slowly smothering him to death. He'll die of cystic fibrosis. Just like his older brother did.

"Josh had no idea it was all about to end," Ben said. "At least I know. And I don't want to spend the time I have left, dying. I want to live my life."

And how do you argue with that?

"How can I help?" I asked him at the same time that Luke said, "I'll go with you."

"I'll come too," Natalie said, even though she shouldn't.

"Me too," Kyle said.

Because this is who we are, the friends who help you do what matters to you, even if it's incredibly stupid.

Ben's face was relieved. "Thanks, guys."

"What will we need?" Natalie said.

"My vest and a way to power it," Ben told us.

"Food," Kyle threw in.

"We'll have to go slowly. So, tents and sleeping bags," Luke said.

"A first aid kit," I added. And hopefully, not a medivac helicopter.

"Why did it have to be a mountain?" I said to Luke an hour later as we cleaned up the kitchen.

"I get the mountain," Luke said.

"Really?"

He nodded. "Two years ago, I was thinking about doing it."

"You wanted to climb Mount Washington?"

"I thought about running it."

Luke has to wear a heart monitor to make sure his heart rate doesn't break 130 when we run. If he ran up Mount Washington, his pulse and blood pressure would go through the roof.

"That could have killed you," I said.

Luke nodded. "That was kind of the idea."

The pot I was holding slipped out of my hands and

fell into the sink, sending a wave of soapy water gushing over the side. "You were going to kill yourself with a mountain?"

Luke offered me a towel, but I didn't take it.

"Why?" I asked him.

Luke crouched down to clean up the water. "It was a bad month."

He thought about it for a month?

"I was tired of waiting for the inevitable," he said. "I wanted to go out on my terms."

"So you were going to kill yourself?"

"I didn't do it."

"But you were thinking about it." Which is almost as bad.

Luke didn't look at me. He had seriously thought about it.

"You aren't climbing Mount Washington with us," I said.

Luke stood up, his forehead furrowed. "What?"

"You aren't climbing the mountain with us."

"And when did that become your call?" Luke said.

"When you lost your mind."

Luke's face hardened. "I haven't lost my mind."

"Trying to kill yourself, by definition, means you've lost your mind."

Luke's voice was rising. "I'm not trying to kill myself."

"But you were thinking about it," I yelled.

I didn't notice Ben and Natalie and Kyle all standing in the kitchen doorway until Kyle muttered, "I hate it when Mom and Dad fight."

"We are not fighting," Luke and I said at the same time.

"They're yelling for the fun of it," Ben said.

Natalie's voice was shaky. "Luke, are you really thinking about—" She couldn't even say it.

"No," Luke said. "Aly's overreacting."

"I am *not* overreacting!" I said. Though it probably would have been more convincing if I hadn't been yelling.

Luke walked out of the kitchen. The others slowly followed him. I banged the pot into the sink again and started scrubbing at it viciously. Luke wanted to die? The thought was unbelievable to me. How could he of all people even think about that? Ben's right. People die suddenly all the time. At least we have forewarning. That's supposed to make us the ones who appreciate life, not end it early.

"I'm pretty sure it's clean," Ben said a few minutes later.

I paused and looked over at him. I hadn't heard him come back into the room.

"I'm sorry," Ben said. "I didn't mean to start something between you guys."

"You didn't."

"Really? Because Luke's scowling, and you're beating up the pots and pans."

I put down the pot and started drying my hands with a towel. If Ben was concerned, I could imagine how much worse Natalie looked.

"I'll come back in," I said.

Ben gave me a little nod—thanks, maybe.

I went into the family room and sat down in my usual chair.

Natalie looked nervously between Luke and me. "How about a movie?"

No one else had any better ideas, so we let the TV fill in the silence.

SATURDAY, JUNE 4

I must have fallen asleep, because I woke up to the sound of my phone dinging. The room was dark except for the changing lights of the TV. The others were all sleeping, stretched out on couches or sprawled in chairs in their funeral clothes. I got up and glanced at the phone as I carried it into the kitchen.

Caroline, 1:14 A.M.: *I thought you were sleeping.*

Me, 1:15 A.M.: *I was.*

Caroline, 1:15 A.M.: *But I just saw you.*

Me, 1:16 A.M.: *No, you didn't. I'm at Luke's.*

Caroline, 1:16 A.M.: *Are you sure?*

Me, 1:16 A.M.: *Yes.*

Caroline, 1:17 A.M.: *But you had on your yellow sweater.*

Me, 1:18 A.M.: *I don't own a yellow sweater. I hate yellow.*

If she had been sober, she would have

remembered that.

Caroline, 1:18 A.M.: *Big Bird is yellow. How can you hate Big Bird?*

Me, 1:19 A.M.: *I didn't say that I hated Big Bird.*

Caroline, 1:20 A.M.: *Big Bird is a* Sesame Street *legend. He has a big-ass nest. You could fit a motorcycle in that nest.*

Me, 1:21 A.M.: *Why would Big Bird park a motorcycle in his nest?*

Caroline, 1:22 A.M.: *I don't know. I think I'm drunk.*

Me, 1:22 A.M.: *Don't drive.*

Caroline, 1:23 A.M.: *I can't. I lost my car.*

Me, 1:23 A.M.: *That's good, because you shouldn't be driving.*

Caroline, 1:24 A.M.: *But I need to get home.*

Me, 1:24 A.M.: *Where are you?*

Caroline, 1:26 A.M.: *Somewhere with lots of solo cups.*

Me, 1:26 A.M.: *That really doesn't help. Why don't you ask someone?*

Caroline, 1:27 A.M.: *Okay.*

Caroline, 1:30 A.M.: *This guy doesn't know.*

Me, 1:30 A.M.: *Why don't you ask someone else?*

Caroline, 1:31 A.M.: *Okay. What was I asking?*

Me, 1:31 A.M.: *Where you are.*

Caroline, 1:32 A.M.: *Right.*

Caroline, 1:37 A.M.: *Bloody hell. I'm at the CIA.*

I leaned my head back against the refrigerator.

Me, 1:37 A.M.: *They don't have a house on campus.*

Caroline, 1:38 A.M.: *Are you sure?*

Me, 1:38 A.M.: *Yes.*

Caroline, 1:39 A.M.: *But the sign on the wall says CA.*

Caroline, 1:40 A.M.: *I'm in freaking California.*

Me, 1:41 A.M.: *You're not in California.*

Caroline, 1:42 A.M.: *Walls don't lie.*

Me, 1:43 A.M.: *Stay there. I'm coming to get you.*

Caroline, 1:44 A.M.: *You're driving all the way to California? You really do love me.*

Me, 1:45 A.M.: *Usually.*

I put on shoes but still had two problems. 1) I had no way of getting to campus. 2) Going to a frat party by yourself is not smart. If Caroline had been there, I would have taken her with me. But Caroline was the one I needed to retrieve. I knew who my second pick would usually be, but we weren't speaking. Natalie was too young, and well, Natalie. And the smoke would be bad for Ben. That left Kyle.

I was pretty sure I was going to regret this, but I knelt next to Kyle's sprawled body.

"Kyle," I whispered. He didn't move. I touched his arm, but he just snored. "Kyle," I said a little louder.

Kyle didn't move. But a voice behind me said, "Aly?"

I looked back to see Luke sitting up. He rubbed the sleep out of his eyes. "What are you doing?"

"Trying to get Kyle to go with me to a frat party."

"Caroline?"

I nodded.

"Leave him. I'll go with you."

"You don't have to."

But Luke was already putting on shoes.

When we were both buckled into his car, Luke said, "Next time just ask me."

"We were fighting."

"You can always ask me. Even when we're fighting."

Luke turned on the car and I said, "I didn't know the rules."

"Are you planning on doing this often enough that we need rules?"

"No. I don't fight with you. I fight with Caroline."

"And you two have rules?" he said.

"We don't hit below the belt, and the fight can't last more than thirty minutes. After that, we have to stop. Even if we don't agree."

"I could live with those rules," Luke said.

"But we're way past thirty minutes."

"Then I guess we agree to disagree."

"You mean I stop trying to stop you."

"Pretty much."

I looked out the window at the streetlights making pools of light on the dark road. "I don't want to lose you."

"I'm not going anywhere."

I looked back at his beautiful, steady face. "But the hike—"

"Is going to be slow. It'll have to be, if we're going to have any chance of getting Ben all the way to the top."

"You promise me you won't run?"

"I promise," Luke said.

"You'll be careful?"

"I'll be careful."

I still didn't like it. But I knew I wasn't going to stop him. And Luke keeps his promises.

I let out a breath I hadn't known I was holding. "Okay."

We turned onto the road that leads into campus, and Luke said, "Which house?"

"Chi Alpha."

He said something that should have been smurfed.

"What's wrong with it?"

"They like to spike the punch."

Of course, Caroline had to end up at that house. I called her, but she didn't answer.

"She probably can't hear it," Luke said.

I wished he would drive faster.

When we made it to the Chi Alpha house, the lawn was

strewn with empty red plastic cups and a few other things I didn't want to identify. The music was loud enough to make the wooden steps of the front porch rattle under our feet. There were people everywhere, leaning on the railing, making out in the corners, laughing uncontrollably.

Once we were inside, Luke yelled, "I'll go left."

I nodded and started moving through the crowd to the right. The room stank of beer and bodies. And more than once I got trapped between groups of people. But I kept pushing my way further and further into the house.

I found Caroline in the kitchen attempting to swallow some guy's tongue. I had to yell before she noticed me and came up for air.

"Hi, Aly," she said. "This is Clark. He's from New Hampshire too."

"Crazy coincidence. Come on. We're leaving."

"No." Caroline's voice dropped to a stage whisper. "He could be The One."

"He's not the one."

Caroline frowned. "How do you know?"

"Because Clark hates Big Bird."

Caroline's head whipped around to glare at Clark. "That is not cool," she said, pushing him away.

Clark stared at us in confusion as I took hold of Caroline's arm and led her back toward the front door. Her steps were unsteady, but I've had plenty of practice at the marionette game of maneuvering a drunk Caroline.

Luke caught up with us by the front door.

"What's on your hands?" I asked him.

"Punch. I flipped it over."

Because he's Luke.

Luke drove. I sat in the back with Caroline, who was starting to look sick.

"You are not throwing up in this car," I told her.

"Then you should probably pull over," Caroline said.

So we ended up parked along the road that leads away from campus while Caroline puked into a bush.

When we made it back to his house, Luke and I got Caroline up the stairs. We laid her on her side on Luke's bed and covered her up with blankets. It felt strangely like tucking in a child, if children smelled like beer and sick.

When we got downstairs, Luke said, "Grilled cheese?"

I hadn't realized I was hungry. But once he mentioned food, I could feel how empty my stomach was. "That would be great."

Luke grilled the sandwiches and slid them onto plates. We went out onto the back porch and sat on the top step to eat.

When the sandwiches were gone, and the quiet had stretched out around us, I had to ask, "Why didn't you?"

"Why didn't I what?" Luke said.

"Why didn't you run up the mountain?"

He didn't answer right away.

"Were you worried about what it would do to your family?" I asked.

"No. I wrote you all letters so you would understand."

He got as far as writing the letters.

"Having one of your kids die is horrible," Luke said. "It doesn't matter when it happens. If anything, me going out on the mountain might have been easier for them. At least that way it would be all at once. They wouldn't have to do the ICU vigil or sign the papers to take me off life support."

I was trying not to picture Luke in an ICU bed. The staff turning off the machines. His chest lying still. His skin turning cold.

"I'd been living with this time bomb in my head for so long. Waking up every day wondering if this was going to be the day that if finally went off. And I couldn't do it anymore. I hated it. I hated what it had done to my family. How much my dad worried and how Mom put her whole life on hold to be with me. I hated that it got to decide when I stopped breathing." He looked at me, needing me to understand.

And I realized that I could. Larry was his Rick, the thing that had stolen his childhood and left him powerless to control his own life. I could understand that.

"So you decided to make the decision yourself," I said.

Luke nodded. "I wrote a letter, telling my parents which trail I was going to take. I was going to do it at night. Just start sprinting full-out up the mountain. When the pressures got too high and Larry burst, at least it would be my choice, not his."

"But you didn't do it."

"No."

"Why?"

Luke looked out at the dark yard. "It takes time to organize Search and Rescue. But you and Caroline weren't going to wait that long. The two of you would have gone looking for me."

We would have.

"You're the runner," he said. "You would have been the one to find me."

I could see it, Luke's body sprawled out on the ground. Me trying CPR, anything I could think of to bring him back. But he was already gone. And I ended up cradling his head in my lap, agony curling my body over his.

Luke was still looking out at the dark lawn when he said, "I love you too much to do that to you."

And everything stopped.

There was no sound or sensation. The entire world was holding its breath.

"You love me?" I whispered.

He looked back at me, his brows furrowed. "I've been in love with you since I was fourteen years old. I thought you knew."

I shook my head. Caroline had known. But I hadn't.

"I always figured it was all over my face," Luke said.

Maybe it was, but I hadn't seen it.

"You never said anything."

Luke leaned forward to rest his arms on his legs. "No, I didn't."

He was in love with me, but he had avoided telling me. Just like he had avoided kissing me. I saw it all over again, the two of us on the lawn behind the Ballentine. The stars lighting up the dark sky. Me leaning in, and Luke pulling back. A fist tightened in my stomach. I wanted to know why, and at the same time I didn't. Because I had a horrible feeling I already knew.

"Because of the HIV?" I whispered.

Luke nodded, and I wanted to die, right there in that moment. To not have to feel anything ever again.

I thought he was different. But even Luke didn't want me.

I stood up, but Luke caught my hand.

"Aly," he said.

"I get it." The words caught in my throat and I hated them for that. But I didn't know why I would expect this moment to be any less horrifying.

"Listen," Luke said.

I didn't want to sit down and listen to Luke Harrison calmly explain how this could never work, that I'm contaminated and deadly, and we could never have a normal life together. I know all that. I know it better than he ever could. I wanted to pull my hand out of his and leave. And maybe I would have if he had tried to force me to stay. But he didn't. His grip was light. He would have let go if I pulled away.

"Please," Luke said.

And I made the mistake of looking at him. I looked down at the boy who became my friend when most of the school was avoiding me, the guy who got into the only fight of his life because of me, the friend who sang "Edelweiss" in an *I ♥ Guinea Pigs* t-shirt just because I asked him to—and I slowly sat back down.

Luke still had my hand. His eyes weren't on the yard now, or the wall of the house. He was looking right at me.

"Aly, I'm not saying I don't want you because of the HIV. I'm saying you shouldn't want *me*."

Which didn't make any sense.

"With the right meds and a little luck, you could live for decades," Luke said. "I don't have that kind of time. I could be dead next week."

"Don't say that."

"But it's true. When this thing in my head goes off, it will be like a bomb. The closer people are when it detonates, the worse the damage."

"I hate that analogy."

"But it's accurate," he said.

"Then I guess I'm doomed."

"But it could be worse. If we get too close, it will be worse."

He didn't get it.

"It can't get any worse," I said. "I'm in love with you."

Luke looked like he couldn't absorb the words. "What?"

I wanted to kiss him. But the thought of him pulling away again was unbearable.

So I reached out, and for the first time in my life, I touched his cheek.

"I'm in love with you," I said again.

And this time I saw the change in his eyes, the surprise, and the wonder.

He believed me.

STILL SATURDAY, JUNE 4

This morning, I woke up in my usual post-funeral chair. That part was normal. So was the sound of the others talking in the kitchen. Even the memory of retrieving Caroline wasn't that strange. But what happened after—I still didn't know what to do with that.

As I sat up, my thoughts went running off in different directions. I could have dreamt the whole thing. Or imagined its significance. Or maybe it had happened the way I remembered, but it had been Luke's way of coping with Josh's death, of reminding himself that he was still alive.

He didn't kiss me. I can't stop remembering that.

He knows the chances of contracting HIV from kissing are microscopic. But there's still a chance. What if it isn't a chance he's willing to take?

What if he doesn't feel the same way about me that I feel about him?

But he said that he loved me. That he's been in love with me since he was fourteen years old. And I couldn't think of a reason why he would tell me that last night, only to reject me this morning.

Unless he had let himself forget who I am, and sleep had reminded him that I'm the girl with HIV. No one should want me.

Luke came into the living room, and I wanted to hide. But he obviously saw me, because he came over to sit on the ottoman in front of my chair.

Last Fourth of July, we all went to the hotel to watch the fireworks. While we were waiting for it to get dark, there was this incredible sunset. The kind that made me long for paints and a canvas. Everyone was looking at the sunset, except for Luke. I caught him looking at me like I was the most astounding thing he had ever seen.

I had convinced myself that it didn't mean anything. That he was really just looking at the sky. But this morning when that same expression came onto his face, there was no sunset. Just me. And all of my doubts about how he felt melted away in the warmth of that smile.

"Did you sleep all right?" he said.

"The two hours I got were magical," I said.

"We should rent the chair out to insomniacs."

"I'm sure they would appreciate it."

He smiled at me. "So, will you have dinner with me tomorrow night?"

"You mean like a date?"

"Exactly like a date."

I only considered for a second before I said, "That would be nice."

I have a date. With Luke Harrison. The idea still hasn't completely sunk in.

Caroline was unconscious when I walked into Luke's room.

I opened the blinds. "Good morning, Sunshine."

Caroline groaned. She started to sit up, but all of the color drained from her face, and she ended up leaning back into the headboard looking sick. I watched her realize where she was, and what must have happened.

"I'm sorry," Caroline said.

"I know. Which is why I didn't bring you a plate of runny eggs."

I handed her water and Motrin instead.

"Thanks." She took the pills before handing me back the glass.

I said, "We're climbing Mount Washington the day after graduation."

"We are?"

"It's on Ben's bucket list."

Caroline pressed her hands against her forehead. "Why couldn't he want to sing on Broadway?"

"I don't know. But he doesn't. Oh, and Luke told me

that he loved me last night."

Caroline dropped her hands to look at me. "What?"

"We had this huge fight about hiking, and then he told me that he loved me."

Caroline shook her head. "Start at the beginning."

So I told her the whole story, from Ben and the mountain, all the way up to this morning and dinner plans.

"You have to admit it," Caroline said.

I rolled my eyes. "You were right."

She grinned.

"Should I yell it from the rooftops?" I asked, raising my voice with each word.

Caroline pressed her hands to her head again. "That's evil, Aly."

But I was too happy to feel guilty.

It was a happiness that lasted for maybe an hour. But by the time I made it back to the Millers', the euphoria was wearing off, and I was starting to think.

This was the beginning of a romantic relationship, something I know nothing about. And it's not with just any guy. It's with Luke.

I called Caroline in a slight panic.

She answered the phone with the words, "You aren't crazy. You took a chance. Taking risks is part of really living."

"You practiced that."

"I had a longer version, but this seemed to get to the point."

"I'm nervous."

"I know," Caroline said.

"When friends date, it doesn't always work out. I don't want to lose Luke."

"I know."

"So what do I do now?"

Caroline said, "There used to be these old cartoons where a coyote would chase a roadrunner off a cliff. And the coyote was fine, until he looked down."

"So?"

"Don't look down."

SUNDAY, JUNE 5

All Luke told me about our date was that it would be casual, so I got dressed in jeans and my favorite shirt. I don't really wear makeup, so I decided not to try and experiment today. I just did my best to cover the shadows under my eyes and put on a little lip gloss.

All I had told the Millers was that Luke was picking me up. My plan was to be ready and waiting on the porch when he got here. But before I got downstairs, I heard the doorbell ring.

I opened my bedroom door as Luke said, "Hello, Mrs. Miller."

By the time I made it to the foyer, Mrs. Miller was staring at the bouquet of peonies Luke was holding.

"This isn't a group dinner?" Mrs. Miller said.

"No," Luke said. "It's a date."

Mrs. Miller's face was baffled. "You're going on a date, with Aly?"

Luke nodded. But as his eyes settled on me, his expression shifted into a smile. "You look beautiful."

"Thank you." I glanced from Luke to the door, and he took the hint.

Luke opened the front door for me as he told Mrs. Miller, "I'll have her back before curfew."

We made it onto the porch, and Luke shut the door before Mrs. Miller could regain the power of speech. He offered me a hand. I hesitated, but only for a second before I slid my hand into his. We walked down the steps together.

"Where are we going?" I asked him.

"Somewhere we haven't been in a long time."

"That really doesn't narrow it down."

"You'll just have to be patient."

Luke drove us out of town and along the Lost River Road. I knew where we were, but not where we were going until he turned onto a dirt service road that ran through the back of the Ballentine property. He parked on a knoll above the hotel, right beside the tool shed that had been our club house when we were kids. The windows were so thick with dust they looked frosted. But the doors stood open, and the light from the setting sun shone on my very first mural. Caroline had wanted something psychedelic. Luke had wanted blue. So I made it a garden. Blue sky for Luke. Bright colors for Caroline. Flowers for me.

Set out in front of the clubhouse was a blanket complete with a basket of food.

"I owe you for the last time we came to the Ballentine," Luke said.

I kicked off my shoes and sat down, feeling the blanket under my hands and the grass under my bare feet. "It was a great night."

Luke sat next to me. "Except for the end."

"Except for that."

Luke moved so I couldn't help but look at his face. "This time, I'm not pulling away. I'm all in."

"I don't know what that means."

"It means I will always love you."

A vise was suddenly clamping down on my chest.

Luke's brows furrowed.

I tried to smile. "That's why my mom spelled my name the way she did. She wanted to call me Aly and have it stand for Always Love You." I shook my head. "I shouldn't have told you that."

"Why?"

"Because I don't want to talk about my mom tonight."

"Okay," he said. "We won't talk about your mom, or my mom, or Mother's Day, or Mother Goose, or anything the least bit mom-related."

"Were you planning on talking about nursery rhymes on our first date?"

"I wasn't planning on it," Luke said. "But you never know when they might come up."

"Sure."

"I'm not mentioning the other thing," Luke said. "But I'm glad you told me about your name."

"Why?"

"Because I'll never say it the same way again. Now every letter has weight. It's more than a name. It's a promise."

And Luke keeps his promises.

After it grew dark, and the stars came out to fill up the sky, Luke kissed me. He kissed me, and I felt like I was coming alive.

I've been in love with Luke for years. But to love him and know that he loves me back is a feeling that I can't describe. It's like Christmas morning, and the first snowfall, and the last day of school, all wrapped up into one.

I can't sleep. But for once it's because I want to remember. I don't want to ever forget the way his thumb traced the edge of my hand, and his voice made the cool air feel warm. And how he smiled at me like I light up his whole world.

MONDAY, JUNE 6

Last night, all I wanted to do was remember. Today, all I wanted to do was forget. Because today I had to go to Boston.

I wanted to go back to talking about meeting Rick in the grocery store. But Mr. Raleigh was flipping back through his notes from my original interviews.

"What happened on Mr. Wallace's birthday?"

I didn't want to talk about that.

I opened the bottle of water sitting in front of me on the table and took a drink. But it didn't really help. I still had to answer the question.

"I made him a card."

"You made a card for the man who was abusing you?" Mr. Raleigh said.

"I didn't know he was abusing me." My hands closed around the bottle. "We had this neighbor in our apartment building, Mrs. Lewendowski. She looked like the witches in books, with wrinkly skin and stringy white hair. I never wanted to go near her. But anytime we saw her, Mama always made me kiss her cheek. She said that sometimes we have to do things we don't like in order to make other people happy. So that's how I thought about Rick touching me. I didn't like it. But it made him happy."

"And you wanted Mr. Wallace to be happy?" Mr. Raleigh said.

"I did. He was good to us. And we lived in his house. Mama wanted to marry him."

And I wanted Rick to keep loving me. I didn't tell Mr. Raleigh that. But it's true. I had never had a man who paid that much attention to me, who made me feel special, and safe. I didn't want to lose that love.

So I made him a birthday card. On the front, I drew a birthday cake. Inside, was a picture of Mama and Rick and me, all holding hands and smiling. We were even wearing party hats.

I gave him my card at dinner that night.

"This is beautiful," Rick said.

And I felt a little surge of happiness. A surge that grew when he said there would be no more after-dinner movies.

"School starts in a few days," Rick said. "And it's time Little Miss started getting to bed on time."

I was so relieved. I thought the bad part was over.

Until he came into my room that night.

I was sitting in bed looking at a book when Rick locked the door and crossed the room. He sat down on the edge of the bed and took the book out of my hands, setting it on my bedside table.

"I loved the card you made me," Rick said. "But it isn't a present. Don't you have a present for me on my birthday?"

I shook my head. I hadn't known I was supposed to make him a present. Mama was always happy with a card.

"It's okay," Rick said. "You don't have to buy me anything. You can give me a different kind of present."

That sounded better, until he said, "Take off your clothes and let me see that beautiful skin."

I froze.

Rick's face moved from happy to deeply disappointed. "I thought you loved me."

"I do," I whispered.

But Rick shook his head. "If you loved me, you would want me to be happy on my birthday."

"I do want you to be happy." I whispered.

But Rick's face didn't believe me. He thought I didn't love him.

My hands were shaking, and my heart was pounding, but I slowly took off my nightgown. The air was cold against my skin, and I hugged the balled-up material to my chest.

Rick smiled as took the protection of the nightgown out of my hands. "Now lay down for me."

I didn't want to do this.

But if I didn't, Rick would stop loving me. And If Rick didn't love us, Mama and I would lose everything. And it would be my fault.

Slowly, I made myself lay down on the bed.

Rick let his eyes slide over my naked body. "Happy birthday to me," he sang quietly as he unbuttoned his pants.

Mrs. Miller was silent as I climbed into the passenger seat of the car. She worked her way through traffic, and I pulled my knees up to my chest, wrapping my arms around my legs. I folded up as tight as I could. But I couldn't keep the memories out. They kept crashing into me.

I gripped my legs so hard that my nails broke through my skin. I should have let go then. But I didn't. I pressed harder, dragging my fingers down a fraction of an inch so that the cuts grew. The pain grew sharper. But I didn't stop. I dug deeper, until I couldn't feel anything but where my fingers were piercing my skin.

Mrs. Miller didn't notice. She was too busy staring out the windshield, her face settled into a tight expression of resentment.

I knew there would be cuts, probably bruises, all things I could cover. If Mrs. Miller had caught me, she would have blown a gasket. The woman is terrified of my blood. But I didn't care. I dug deeper and let the pain do its job. It drowned out the fear, the horror, the memories.

For a little while it even took away the shame.

TUESDAY, JUNE 7

This morning when Luke picked me up for school, he got out of the car to kiss me.

"How was yesterday?" he said.

Horrifying. But I couldn't say that. He still thinks I'm going to Boston for mentoring. So I told him, "Okay."

When we were both in the car, Luke said, "Mom and Dad want to have you over for dinner tonight."

"You told them about us?"

Luke nodded. "Saturday morning. Why do you look nervous?"

"This is dinner with your parents. Isn't that supposed to make me nervous?"

"Meeting the parents is supposed to make you nervous. But you already know them. You've seen them sing showtunes in the kitchen."

That's true. But this still felt different.

Luke and I have been on a date. We're dating. Tonight might even count as a second date. I would have to check the legal definition. Either way, this isn't just dinner at my friend's house. This is dinner with the parents of the guy I'm dating. That brought up all kinds of possible pitfalls, starting with the fact that I had no idea what to wear. There should be an agreed upon fashion rating system for social events. Then every invitation could come with a number. But in the meantime, I had to figure it out for myself.

I finally decided on a blue sundress, because it seemed to be the right degree of casual, and Luke told me once that he liked it. But once I had the dress on, I couldn't help but notice how much skin was showing. The skirt of the dress is long, but my arms and shoulders were bare. I've never thought of the dress as inappropriate before. But I've also never been dating a minister's son before.

I'm dating a minister's son. I still can't get used to that idea.

To a small town, there is nothing more delicious than gossiping about the minister's family. They're going to find out we're dating. And they're going to have a field day.

And what about Luke's parents? What did they really think about their son dating the girl with HIV? Luke's mother used to teach nursing at the University of New Hampshire. She knows how much of a risk I am to him. She can't want me anywhere near her baby. If she got me alone, would she be polite about it, or just tell me to stay away from her son?

It took a force of will to make me leave the house and walk the three blocks to the Harrisons'. I kept envisioning one of Luke's parents slamming the door in my face. But when the Harrisons' door opened, it was Luke standing on the other side. He smiled when he saw me, but the smile didn't last.

"Are you okay?" Luke said, taking in the skirt that reached down to my feet and the heavy sweater I had added for coverage.

"I'm fine."

But his brows furrowed. "It's almost eighty degrees, and you're dressed for the arctic. Are you running a fever?"

I shook my head, but he reached out to touch me anyway. His hand rested against my cheek for mere seconds, but it was long enough to send warmth rushing to the spot.

"You don't feel feverish," Luke said. "But now your cheeks are getting pink."

Which made the heat intensify. I was blushing about blushing because he touched my cheek.

Luke took my hand. "We need to find a thermometer."

"Luke, I'm fine."

"If you have a fever, that's serious."

Fevers are concerning for anyone whose immune system might be compromised. But I wasn't running a fever; unless a temperature spike based on embarrassment counts. Still, I knew that nothing short of a normal temperature was going to satisfy him. So I let him take my hand and lead me into the house, then up the stairs.

Luke took me as far as his room. "Give me a second."

He let go of my hand and walked down the hall toward the bathroom. I went into Luke's room to wait.

I've always liked Luke's room. The walls are a deep navy blue. There's a big chair, with his guitar resting in a stand beside it. On the opposite wall are bookcases stuffed full of books and Iron Man lunchboxes.

When Luke was seven, he wanted an Iron Man lunchbox. His mom went to all the local stores, but they were sold out. When she told him they would get him one next year, Luke yelled, "I could die before then," and ran upstairs and cried in his closet. He said it was the first time he ever really freaked out about dying. His mom found him an Iron Man lunchbox. And she still buys him one every year. He has eleven of them on his shelves. Sometimes they'll be stacked in pillars or all lined up in a row. Today they made up a pyramid worthy of the Valley of the Kings.

Luke came back with a thermometer that he handed me. Seconds later, it beeped.

He took it back to check the reading. "98.9."

"Which is normal."

"But that doesn't explain how flushed you were on the porch. Or the clothes."

"I was worried."

He was watching me intently. "Worried about what?"

"That my dress wasn't right."

"So you wore a blanket with buttons?"

"It's my sick sweater."

"But you're not sick," Luke said. "We've established that."

He was waiting for proof that I was fine. So I undid the buttons and slowly peeled off the protection of my sweater.

"What's wrong with the dress?" Luke said.

"I thought maybe it didn't cover enough."

"It's a sundress. It's perfect."

Luke took my sweater and put it on his desk chair. "So why were your cheeks hot on the porch?"

"That was your fault."

He frowned slightly. "All I did was ask if you were all right."

"And you touched me."

Luke's eyes were amused. "All of this because I touched your cheek?"

"It isn't funny."

"I'm not laughing," he said. "I'm wondering."

My voice was so quiet it surprised me. "Wondering what?"

"If you minded."

I shook my head. "It felt nice."

"Good."

I could feel my pulse as Luke slowly reached out to touch me again. This time, he didn't lay his hand against my skin. He used his thumb to trace the curve of my cheek and the edge of my jaw. His touch was so light. But it was setting off another wave of sensation—until Mrs. Harrison's voice called down the hall.

"Luke, did Aly make it?"

Luke dropped his hand as his mother came into the room.

"Oh, Aly, you're here." Mrs. Harrison smiled.

"She's worried about her dress," Luke said.

Mrs. Harrison looked me up and down. "The dress is darling. Luke, can you light the grill before your father blows it up?"

"Sure," he said.

Mrs. Harrison smiled at me. "Aly can help me."

I've always liked Luke's mom, but it still felt strange to follow her downstairs. And even stranger when the front door opened and Luke's older brother Matt walked into the house with a girl.

Matt is finishing his junior year at the University of New Hampshire. I've known him as long as I've known Luke. But the girl was new.

I hung back as Mrs. Harrison hugged her oldest son and was introduced to his date, Kara.

"Hi, Aly," Matt said when he had moved past his mother. He hugged me. "You look pretty."

"Thanks."

"Kara," Mrs. Harrison was saying, "This is Luke's girl-friend, Aly. Aly, Kara."

"Hi," we said to each other.

"Girlfriend?" Matt mouthed at his mother.

"Since Friday night," Mrs. Harrison mouthed back.

Kara and I looked at each other, not knowing what to say. The awkwardness was broken when Luke and his dad came into the room. There were more hugs, more introductions. It was a relief when Luke took my hand again.

"That bad?" Luke whispered when the others were all talking to each other.

"Your mom introduced me as your girlfriend," I whispered.

"I'm pretty sure that's the right word," Luke whispered back.

I blinked at him. "We've been on one date."

"Are you dating anyone else?"

"No."

"Neither am I. Which makes us exclusive—hence the term girlfriend."

We're exclusive.

I liked knowing that Luke wasn't dating anyone else. But at the same time, it felt strange to be exclusive. Almost like I belonged to him.

At dinner, Mrs. Harrison said, "So Luke got some news today."

I turned to look at him. "What news?"

"Just a letter."

"From Dartmouth," Mrs. Harrison said. "They've taken him off the waitlist."

"They offered you a place?" I said.

He nodded.

"That's amazing."

"Congratulations," Matt said.

"I haven't decided if I'm going," Luke said.

"Of course, you're going," Mrs. Harrison said.

"The decision is Luke's." His dad's tone made it clear that this wasn't the first time they'd had this conversation.

"It's an amazing opportunity," Mrs. Harrison said.

"That would be wasted on me," Luke said.

Mrs. Harrison looked ready to delve into round two, but Luke turned to Kara. "Has Matt told you about my head?"

Kara glanced at Matt before she nodded.

"So you get why I'm not going?"

Kara clearly didn't know what to say.

"Luke." His father said. "You are making her uncomfortable."

Luke looked at Kara. "I'm sorry."

She nodded.

"I just don't see the point in going to college when we all know I won't finish."

"Maybe we should wait on this conversation," Luke's dad said.

"There isn't anything to talk about," Luke and his mother said at almost the same time.

And an awkward silence fell over the table.

Luke didn't say anything as he walked me back to the Millers' after dinner. And I didn't ask. I figured he would talk to me when he was ready. When we got to the Millers' front porch, I was expecting him to walk me to the door and then leave. But he sat down on the porch steps. So I sat down next to him.

"It would be pointless," he said. "But Mom can't see that."

"She wants you to be happy."

"She doesn't want to face reality."

"She's your mom. You can't blame her for that."

Luke let out a breath and nodded.

"I don't want to face reality either," I told him.

He looked at me, the tension disappearing from his face. Instead his expression became half worried, half resigned. "You changed your mind about us."

"I haven't changed my mind about anything." My throat was getting tight. "I'm just not ready to lose you."

Luke wrapped his arms around me. "I'm right here."

For now.

When the porchlights flashed, I looked at the time. "I've got to go in."

Luke stood up and offered me a hand.

I didn't have to look to know that Mrs. Miller was watching us through a window. Luke apparently didn't notice or didn't care. Because he leaned in and kissed me.

"Goodnight, Aly," he said.

"Goodnight."

When I walked into the house, Mrs. Miller was waiting for me in the foyer.

"We need to talk," she said.

Which is never a good sign.

I followed her into the family room where Mr. Miller was watching TV. He turned it off when we came in. Mrs. Miller sat next to her husband and pointed at a chair on the other side of the room. I sat down, unsure what I should be bracing myself for.

"How was dinner?" Mrs. Miller said.

"Um, nice." Mostly.

"Did you behave yourself?" Mr. Miller said.

I wasn't sure what he meant by that. I had been polite and offered to help with the dishes and thanked the Harrisons for having me. But that apparently wasn't what the Millers were concerned about.

"Did you keep your knees together?" Mr. Miller said.

It took me a second to realize what he meant. Understanding brought all of the heat from my body rushing into my face.

"I'm not sleeping with Luke," I said.

The Millers studied me, as if they were trying to decide if I was lying.

"And I'm not planning on starting."

Mrs. Miller said, "You remember what Dr. Jordan told us. There is no safe sex for you. Condoms break."

"I know."

"You could infect him," Mrs. Miller said. "And the last thing that sweet boy needs is to catch your disease."

He's a sweet boy. I don't want to know what they think I am.

The lecture went on for what felt like hours. But my thoughts were only loosely connected to what they were saying.

I love Luke. Did they really think I would ever take a chance of giving him HIV? How selfish do they think I am?

They know how much this disease has put a shadow on my life. Or they would, if they paid attention. Of course, if they paid attention, they would probably also know that I have no interest in sex, at all. The most traumatic events of my life involved sex. I can't imagine anything more horrifying than having to do that again.

It was when they had let me go and I had made it to my room that another thought crashed into me.

I don't have any interest in sex. But what if Luke does? What if he wants to have sex with me?

I couldn't breathe. Panic was flooding my lungs, driving out all of the air.

I had to force myself to take deep breaths, to try and think.

Luke doesn't believe in casual sex. We've talked about that.

And he knows about my HIV. He shouldn't want me like that.

But he's eighteen and male. According to the cover of every magazine in the grocery store checkout line, he thinks about sex almost constantly. And he's dying. What does HIV matter when you're already running out of time?

I was desperately trying to convince myself that no one could ever want me like that. That I'm too filthy and broken. But that caused a stab of pain to mix in with my panic.

Either Luke wants to have sex with me, which is horrifying.

Or he doesn't, because I'm dirty and contaminated, and that's crushing.

I am in so far over my head.

WEDNESDAY, JUNE 8

All day, my head has been full of desperate confused thoughts. It was a relief to get to the mural room and close the doors on everything else. I set up my palette the way I always do, from left to right, Titanium White to Onyx Black, today adding an especially large pool of Cadmium Red. Because today I was working on Little Red Riding Hood. I mixed the shades I would need, from a deep merlot all the way to the lightest blush. When everything was ready, I started to paint.

Little Red Riding Hood wasn't a main character in the mural, just a glimpse of red tucked between the trees. Just enough to catch the eye of a wolf.

I was so immersed in my work that I didn't even notice Luke until he was halfway across the room.

"What are you doing here?" I said, putting down my palette and brush.

Luke wrapped his arms around me. "I missed you."

"You dropped me off an hour ago."

"I can miss you in an hour," he said.

"I'm that missable?"

"You're highly missable."

He leaned in, and I kissed him.

At first, I was going through the motions, my mind still caught up in other things. But then slowly those thoughts were fading, and I was feeling more than thinking. Feeling Luke's lips, and the warmth that was spreading through me. I didn't know how a kiss could be this gentle and this passionate at the same time. I just knew I liked how it felt.

Until his fingers slid into my hair.

Rick's hand twisted through my hair, forcing my head where he wanted it to go. Panic exploded in my mind. And then I was stumbling backwards. The yellow bedroom was gone. I was in the mural room. My breaths were coming too fast, my heart beating too hard, the desperation so overwhelming I thought I was going to be sick.

"Aly?"

I took a step toward Luke's voice and felt his arms wrap around me. Pressing my face into his shirt, I struggled to breathe.

Luke held me tighter. "It's okay."

Slowly, my heart rate came down, and my breaths lost their ragged edges. The dread was still lingering, but it was manageable.

"Did I do something wrong?" Luke said.

I leaned back enough to make sure he could see my face. "No. You didn't do anything wrong."

"Then what happened?"

I couldn't tell him about the flashback. But I couldn't add another layer of lies either. So I told him another truth.

"Last night, when I went inside, the Millers ambushed me about sex. Was I sleeping with you already, or was I going to start, and did I know how risky that was? They think you don't need my disease on top of everything else."

Understanding overtook the concern on Luke's face.

"And then I kiss you like that, and you start worrying about what I was planning," Luke said.

I nodded.

"I was planning on kissing you. And then sitting on that pile of drop cloths and talking to you while you paint."

Genuine relief eased away a layer of anxiety I hadn't even known I had. "That was it?"

"That was it."

He tilted his head, studying me. "I'm not Troy, and this isn't Truth or Dare."

I froze. I never told him or Caroline about that night.

"Madison told me a couple of months ago," Luke said. "She still feels bad about it."

"It was years ago."

Luke is usually the calm voice of reason. But today, the look on his face was almost frightening. "Which is good. Because I can't kill him now for something he did when he was thirteen."

"It was just a kiss."

"No." Luke's voice was deadly serious. "It wasn't. Troy forced you into something you didn't want. That's assault, not a kiss."

It had all the characteristics of a kiss: lips pressed up against lips, mouths open, our eyes were even closed. Mine because I didn't want to watch, Troy's because he probably didn't want to look at the infectious girl he was kissing.

But Luke was right. Troy hadn't given me a choice. And Luke knew that.

"Is that why you always pause before you kiss me? To give me time to choose?"

He nodded. "Or run screaming from the room."

"I'm not going to run screaming from the room."

Luke looked right into my eyes. "And nothing is ever going to happen between us that you don't want."

He said that as if he was reminding me of a fact I should already know—that it was a universal truth that I should get to decide what my body gets involved in.

When I was little, I used to think of my body as mine, the same way I thought of my name as mine. But every time Rick used it or hurt it, my body felt less and less like it belonged to me. I had no power to control what happened to it. So it couldn't be mine in any way that really mattered. My body was just a place where I lived, a place where terrible things happened.

And over time I came to hate it. It was my body Rick wanted. My body that had to be punished. And my body that won't stop remembering.

Before Mr. Raleigh showed up at the Millers' door, I was doing a pretty good job of chasing every Rick-related thought out of my head. But my body still remembered. And out of nowhere I would suddenly feel it happening again.

I'm supposed to love my body. That's what the books all say. But I don't. And Luke wouldn't either if he knew what it had done.

MONDAY, JUNE 13

"Remember that next week's deposition will be Thursday, not Monday," Mr. Raleigh said as we sat down today.

"Why?" I asked him.

"Thursday worked better for the defense team's schedule."

I was trying not to think about testifying in front of Rick's lawyers. But today, Mr. Raleigh's questions weren't much better.

He opened his notes before he looked at me across the table. "Did you ever tell anyone about the abuse?"

"I tried to tell my mother once."

"When was that?"

"The morning after Rick's birthday."

Mr. Raleigh nodded. "Tell me about it."

When I woke up that morning, everything hurt. And I couldn't stop remembering what had happened.

After it was finally over, Rick had just held me while I cried. His voice was gentle when he said. "It won't hurt so much next time."

Panic turned my voice into a whisper. "Next time?"

Rick nodded. "God, I wish you had been a good girl and kept your clothes on." He was breathing hard. "Because now that I've had a taste, I can't stop." His voice was low and rough.

I was so scared of that happening again, that I was willing to try almost anything, even telling Mama.

So that morning, I made myself get out of bed and go downstairs. I found her in the kitchen scrambling eggs. I went over and wrapped my arms around her legs, holding on as tight as I could.

Mama patted my head. "Morning, baby." But when minutes went by and I still hadn't let go, she pulled me off her. "What's wrong?"

I couldn't tell her that I had taken off my clothes and laid down on the bed for Rick. I was too ashamed. I was praying that Mama didn't have to know about that part. That she would protect me. But first I had to find a way to explain what Rick had done. I did my best, and then I waited.

I hadn't realized I was holding my breath until Mama's face turned angry. Then I could breathe. Because if she was mad about what Rick had done, I knew she wouldn't let him do it again. I was sure that everything was going to be all right—until she grabbed my arm so hard it hurt.

"What is the matter with you?" Mama hissed, her face twisted with disgust. "Are you trying to ruin everything?"

"No."

"Then stop lying."

"I'm not lying. He took off his pants—"

"Stop it!" Mama snapped. "That never happened."

I was crying. "It did, last night in my bed."

Mama dragged me out of the kitchen and down the hall. In the bathroom, she trapped me against the sink. With one hand she pried my lips apart. With the other, she filled my open mouth with the liquid soap we used to wash our hands. I sputtered and gagged, but Mama clasped a hand over my mouth to keep it all inside.

"Rick is the best thing that ever happened to us," Mama said in a tight voice. "And I won't let you ruin it by telling lies."

In the mirror, I saw her livid face and my pale one. And then a tall shape was filling up the doorway. I gasped, and soap filled my nose.

"What's going on?" Rick said.

Mama straightened up and let go of my mouth. It took her a few seconds to clear her face. "I caught Alyson telling a lie."

Rick raised an eyebrow. "That's very serious."

"I know." Mama looked back at me with a tight expression. "I washed her mouth out with soap."

"It takes more than soap to keep a child from turning into a liar," Rick said.

Mama looked at him as if he was the fount of all wisdom. "What do you think I should do?"

He looked thoughtful for a few seconds before he said, "I could punish her for you."

My chest was caving in. I couldn't breathe.

"You would do that?" Mama said.

"It's a father's responsibility to discipline his child."

Mama's face was overwhelmed with love. "You want to be Alyson's father?"

"I do," he said. "If you want me."

"Of course," Mama said. "Of course, we want you."

She reached up to kiss him.

"Why don't you go work on breakfast," Rick said. "I'll take care of this."

Mama nodded. She was going to leave me.

"Please, Mama." I was begging her. "He's going to hurt me."

"Because you deserve it," Mama snapped. And then she walked out of the room.

Rick shut the bathroom door and locked it. Mama's footsteps disappeared down the hall.

She left me.

Sitting in Mr. Raleigh's conference room, I could smell burned eggs, and taste soap, and hear her walking away.

"Have you ever told anyone else?" Mr. Raleigh said.

I shook my head. "Not on purpose. The police found out because of an accident. They made me tell you. But I've never told my friends. Not even my boyfriend."

I couldn't. I would remember Mama leaving me. And I just couldn't say the words.

My first day of Kids' Group, when I had to tell them my diagnosis, most of the kids didn't know what HIV was. But a boy named Marcus did.

"That's the sex disease," he said.

I saw the looks on the kids' faces, and I knew I couldn't tell them I got HIV from having sex with a grown man. I panicked and words came rushing out of my mouth. "That's not how I got it. I got it from my birth mother, and then she died and I went into foster care."

It was what Mrs. Miller had told the school. It was her lie first, but I repeated it. I made it my lie.

The kids looked at me like I had the world's worst luck. And maybe I did. Because I had just lied to Luke and Caroline, who would become my best friends. And as each of our friends joined Group, Luke and Caroline passed on the story. Now they all believe it. And they have for years.

There have been so many moments when I've wanted to tell them the truth. But I could never seem to find the right words. And the more time that went by, the harder it got.

Now I've been lying to them for almost a decade. And how can a relationship possibly survive that?

Dear Olivia,

For most of my life I've been dealing with the same nightmares, the same secrets, the same shame.

And I'm so tired, Olivia.

I wish I could trade my problems in for something else. Something we're actually allowed to talk about.

You can talk about HIV. But when you do, everyone is secretly wondering how you got it. If it was your fault.

Abuse is harder.

The door wasn't completely shut the day my social worker presented my case to the Millers. The Millers had all kinds of questions about HIV and if I would be safe to have in the house. But when my social worker started to tell them how I contracted it, the Millers didn't want to hear that part.

It isn't just the Millers. Society as a whole has unspoken rules.

The topic of sexual abuse is uncomfortable and should be avoided wherever possible.

If you have to mention it, speak in generalities.

Specifics are too disturbing. You will need to keep those to yourself.

They don't think about what it does to us, to keep it all inside, to be trapped in our own heads with the same details they can't bear to think about.

So, I think I would rather have cystic fibrosis.

Either way, I'm slowly suffocating.

At least with cystic fibrosis it wouldn't be a secret.

-Aly

TUESDAY, JUNE 14

Tonight was graduation.

We survived the "Pomp and Circumstance", the welcome, and the valedictorian's speech. But when the principal announced there had been a tie for salutatorian, so both graduates would be giving speeches, Caroline slumped over onto my shoulder and groaned.

We have a long-standing belief that valedictorian and salutatorian speeches should be banned. In part because having the highest GPA in your graduating class doesn't mean you're a decent public speaker. And mostly because they all say the same things. We call it The Formula.

You start with "My fellow graduates." Then you move into the Mad Libs section. "During our four years at Regional High School, [teacher name] taught us [something about their subject], and [teacher name] taught us [something about their subject], but what we really learned was: [choose one of the following: perseverance, how to work together, or the importance of community]."

Paragraph two is an attempt at a joke or funny story.

If anyone has died, they're mentioned here.

The "we can change the world" section is optional.

But the speech has to close with an inspiring quote, or in the case of Liam Winfield, five inspirational quotes. His mother had given him a book of quotes, and he couldn't narrow it down to just one.

When we got through Salutatorian #2, it was time for the diplomas. We tracked Luke's progress as he left his row of chairs and joined the line. Apparently, we weren't the only ones who were paying attention. Because when Luke stepped up onto the stage, the entire crowd got to its feet. The cheers were deafening.

Luke's parents had their arms around each other, and tears running down their cheeks. They hadn't thought they would ever see this day.

Honestly, I hadn't either.

Two years ago, the situation with Luke's head had gotten bad. It was the month he almost ran up the mountain. Instead, he convinced his parents to let him get a shunt placed. If it works, a shunt relieves some of the pressure in the patient's head. In a case like Luke's, it can buy him time. But the procedure is risky. It can lead to permanent brain damage or death.

Caroline and I were waiting outside of the Pediatric ICU when they brought Luke out of the OR. I saw all the tubes and wires, and I was petrified. It was a feeling that didn't get any better a few hours later when his parents came out, and Mrs. Harrison was crying.

"He's dead," I whispered.

Caroline was gripping my hand so tightly she had cut off my circulation.

"No," Reverend Harrison said. "But he may be a little more childlike than he was before. We won't know how extensive the damage is for a few days."

The Harrisons had made arrangements for us to visit. So Caroline and I washed our hands and walked toward Luke's bed, bracing ourselves for what we were going to find. Luke's head was still wrapped up like a Q-tip and his skin was pale. Too many wires connected him to the machines beside his bed. But he saw us, and he smiled.

"Hi." His voice was croaky.

Caroline looked at the TV. "*Curious George*?"

She didn't look at me, and I was grateful. I was having a hard enough time keeping it together.

"Yeah," Luke said. "The remote is stuck. I couldn't change the channel."

Caroline stared at Luke for a second before she said, "What's seven times eight?"

"Fifty-six," he said and then gave me a look that asked what was going on.

But Caroline and I were so relieved we had started laughing uncontrollably. It took us minutes to regain the power of speech.

"Your parents think you have brain damage because you were watching *Curious George,*" I told him.

We still laugh about it. But the shunt did its job. It bought him time—enough time to walk across that stage and receive his diploma.

When the ceremony was over, Luke didn't stop to talk to any of the people who tried to catch his attention. He worked his way through the crowd to us. Luke threw one arm around me and the other around Caroline and pulled us in close. It was the happiest hug I can remember, even before Luke kissed me.

I saw the flashes and looked over. Mrs. Harrison, Mrs. Reese, and Natalie were all taking pictures of the three of us with our arms around each other. Mrs. Harrison showed me some of the pictures later. In my favorite, Caroline is laughing, my whole face is lit up with a smile, and Luke is kissing my cheek.

I'm working not to think about what's coming. Instead, I'm holding onto that image. Because this is how I want to remember us, together and happy.

WEDNESDAY, JUNE 15

Yesterday, Luke graduated from high school.

Today, Ben started up his mountain.

The six of us met in the parking lot at the foot of Mount Washington all dressed alike: t-shirts and shorts, thick socks and hiking boots. My hiking clothes were all borrowed from Caroline. So my socks had pink and blue stripes, and my jacket had the Ballentine crest stitched into the fabric.

"Everyone has pants and jackets?" Luke said.

We all nodded.

When you grow up in these mountains, there are certain things you know. You know that if you get lost in these woods, it's your responsibility to find your way out again. And you know that Mount Washington's weather is notorious. Some of the strongest winds in history were recorded here. And it isn't unheard of to have blizzards hit the top in the middle of the summer. Smart people respect this mountain.

"You're sure you want to do this?" Natalie asked Ben.

"Yes."

"They have a railroad that goes up to the top," Caroline said.

Ben's face was patient, but his voice was firm. "I want to climb it."

So we all picked up our packs.

Ben set our pace, which was painfully slow. But we had expected that. It's why we didn't take the Tuckerman Ravine Trail, that is always crowded with hikers. Instead, we picked the Boott Spur Trail. It's a little longer, has fewer travelers and better vistas. We knew this was going to take a few days, so we figured we might as well enjoy the view.

"Last night at graduation, I kept thinking, that's going to be us next year," Caroline said.

Caroline is one of those irritating people who gets A+'s without trying. The only flaw on her otherwise perfect scholastic record is a zero on a chemistry lab, because she didn't listen to all of the directions and ended up accidentally making hydrogen sulfide. The smell was so horrible people started getting sick, and they had to evacuate an entire wing of the school.

"Your speech will be better than the ones last night," I said.

"If I have to give one, it will definitely be shorter," Caroline said. "Maximum three sentences."

"'I came. I saw. I conquered,' isn't very inspirational."

"How about, 'Take chances. Eat dessert first. Always add sprinkles'?"

"Better."

Natalie fell back to walk with us. "What are we doing?"

"Helping Caroline write an abbreviated graduation speech."

"Oh, I love this." Natalie was thoughtful before she spoke. "Love is worth the risk."

"We have a new graduation speech to beat," Caroline said loudly enough that everyone else turned to look at her. "Nat is leading with five words. Who can do better?"

"What are Nat's five words?" Ben said.

"Love is worth the risk."

Ben thought for a few seconds before he said, "Life is worth living."

"Oh," Caroline and I said together.

Caroline lifted up her arms to get everyone's attention. "Draft 2. Love is worth the risk. Living is worth the cost. Ice cream is worth the calories."

I shook my head. "You had to get dessert in there."

"The speech is supposed to be personal," Caroline said.

And I smiled at her.

When we stopped to let Ben and Natalie rest, or so he could do the vest treatments that shake loose the crud in his lungs, we tried to pick spots with a pretty view. And while we waited, I broke out my pencils. I sketched mountains and valleys, the peeling white bark of the birch trees, and the tender shoots of wildflowers.

These woods have a peacefulness that seeps into you. It must have been getting to Kyle too. Because he waited with the rest of us. And when Ben was ready, Kyle helped to haul him up to his feet.

After lunch, Ben's color was good. But Natalie was too pale.

"Why don't we stay here for a while?" Luke said.

"I'm sorry," Natalie said. "I didn't want to slow you down."

Caroline took the pack out of Natalie's hand. "No, this is good. The longer we stretch out this trip, the less time I have to spend condemned to the laundry room."

Caroline's mom wants her to work every job the Ballentine offers. Last summer, she was a dishwasher. This summer, it's the laundry. By next year, she should have worked her way up to housekeeping.

Ben pulled out a deck of cards, and we all settled down on the ground with Natalie leaning back against a tree trunk.

"Blind Man's Bluff," Ben said. "Aces high."

Caroline grabbed two bags of M&M's from her pack. "Plain are 1000s. Peanut, 5000s." She handed out the goods.

Ben dealt us each one card, face down. On the count of three, we flipped our cards up against our foreheads. Bets were placed and then cards compared. High card wins.

The game is fast. The poker chip equivalents are delicious. And we always laugh a lot. Because everybody looks funny with a card stuck to their forehead.

When Natalie was looking better, we picked up our packs and continued our slow progress up the mountain.

Luke had humored me and wore his heart rate monitor. Every couple of hours, he stretched out his arm so I could read the display on his watch. His heart rate didn't even break a hundred.

Luke might have been fine, but by four o'clock, Ben and Natalie were both fading. So, we decided to stop for the day.

There aren't any huts along this part of the trail, so we looked for a clearing. We ended up finding a spot that has obviously welcomed hikers before. And you can see why. The clearing is large enough for our tents, within earshot of a stream, and has an amazing view.

As we all dropped our packs, Luke said, "Nat, can you stay with Ben and get him to rest?"

Natalie nodded and went over to sink down beside Ben.

"Kyle, can you give me a hand with the tents?" Luke said.

"I can give you one," Kyle said.

Luke looked at me and Caroline. "We need to fill up the canteens and find some firewood."

"We're on it," I told him.

"We are?" Caroline said.

"Yes." I handed her a canteen.

When we were out of sight of the camp, Caroline said, "Natalie looks worse than Ben."

"I know. I'm hoping some rest will help."

Caroline gave me a doubtful look.

"It can't hurt," I said.

When we got back with full canteens and arms full of sticks, Ben and Natalie were looking slightly more human. The tents were up. And Luke was ready to build a fire.

Our campsite was temporarily transformed into a mobile clinic when Ben got out his equipment, and Nat and I pulled out our portable pharmacies. By the time we were all medicated, dinner was cooked. And while we ate macaroni and cheese, the sky took out its paintbox. Soon the clouds were a deep inky blue against the fading light. I wanted to paint that sky; but I didn't have the supplies. So, I had to just sit and enjoy it. The sight was beautiful enough to bring quiet to our circle—at least for a minute.

Then Caroline was suggesting ghost stories. And Natalie discovered that the graham crackers were gone, and the marshmallows were squished. Kyle admitted to eating the graham crackers but vehemently denied squishing the marshmallows, at least on purpose. Luke convinced Natalie that the shape of the marshmallows doesn't matter once they're melted. But Caroline pointed out that without graham crackers, these were going to be the messiest s'mores in the history of s'mores.

But eventually, things settled down, and we started telling stories. Adults may have accomplishments that speak to the fact that they were here. But a lot of the kids who pass through our Group never make it that far. So we remember them in stories. If we manage to get Ben to the top of this mountain, it will be another story to add to the collection.

Tonight, Kyle told the story of Clark Manning, who was in a wheelchair because of osteosarcoma, but still managed to save his younger brother from drowning.

And Natalie told the story of Victoria Pellum, who survived leukemia and went on to become a pediatric oncologist so she could help the next generation of kids fight cancer.

Then Luke started the story of Alyssa Evans. It isn't like the others. Because we always tell this one in parts. The first time we did it this way, it was to humor Natalie. Now I can't imagine telling it any other way.

"Alyssa Evans decided to write a novel," Luke said.

Natalie was the next in the circle. "It told the story of how she wished her life had turned out."

"But before she could finish it, she was too sick to write," Ben said.

"So her friends held a meeting, and they decided to finish the book," Kyle said.

Caroline said, "Each one wrote a chapter with a different way that the story could end."

"And then they each read Alyssa their chapter, and let her choose the ending," I said.

Dr. Klein has a copy of the finished book. But I don't think any of us have ever read it. Because it isn't the ending that matters. It's what her friends did for her that we always remember.

We all went to bed. I lay in my sleeping bag for what felt like hours before I finally gave up on trying to sleep. I put a flannel shirt on over my t-shirt, got my journal and a pen out of my bag, and crawled out of our tent. It took me a few minutes to resurrect the fire. Once it was crackling happily again, I sat down to write.

I had already written the story of the day. And nothing new had happened since I went to bed. So, I was staring at the empty pages, wondering what I was going to write over the next few weeks, when I heard a stick break. I whipped around and then stopped. A shadow of a man was standing on the other side of the clearing.

My heart was suddenly sprinting, and my hands were shaking. But I couldn't move. Cold had dropped through my body, freezing me in place. His shadow was filling up my doorframe. Desperation was building up in my stomach.

Rick closed the door and locked it. He started walking across the room toward me, and tears started sliding down my cheeks.

The room was dark, except for the fairy princess nightlight that made monster shadows on the yellow walls. I knew what I was supposed to do, and what Rick would do to me if I didn't. But I still hesitated. Because a small part of me died every time I had to do this.

Slowly, I got out of bed and stood on the cold floor. With trembling fingers, I started unbuttoning my nightgown.

Usually, Rick just watched and waited while I took off my clothes. But tonight, he did something he had never done before. He said, "Couldn't sleep?"

Only the voice wasn't Rick's.

I felt like I was waking up from a dream. I wasn't in that dark yellow room. I was in a forest. My flannel shirt was half unbuttoned. But the rest of my clothes were where they should be. And there was no sign of Rick. It was Luke standing in front of me in the dark.

"Aly, you're shaking," Luke said. "Are you cold?"

I was thinking words, but my mouth wouldn't form them.

Luke pulled off his sweatshirt. "Here. Put this on."

An ache overwhelmed my chest. He was giving me clothes.

I pulled on the sweatshirt. It was warm from his body heat, and even smelled like him. Like sunshine and coffee and men's body wash.

"Thanks," I managed.

"Come on." He motioned toward the fire.

We sat down next to each other. I had managed to wipe the tears off my face as I pulled on the sweatshirt. But I was still shaky and probably pale. Hopefully, the low light would cover that.

"Why are you up so late?" I asked him.

Luke's voice was amused. "It's nine-thirty."

"The girls are out cold."

"Ben and Kyle too. They're definitely not used to hiking."

It was just the two runners who were awake.

You could tell him what happened, said a small voice in my head.

We were alone. And it was unlikely that any of the others would wake up before morning. I had time. And I had Luke. I leaned over, and he put an arm around me. That helped. So did the warmth of the fire and the layers of clothes.

But to tell him about the memory, I would have to tell him about Rick and the lie. I would have to tell him what I did.

I could feel the shame on my skin. Shame that won't ever wash away.

He would never be able to look at you the same way again, Rick's voice whispered through my head. *He would be too disgusted.*

And I could picture it, the same look of disgust I had seen on my mother's face.

Maybe I should have told Luke.

But I couldn't bring myself to do it.

I just let him hold me and didn't say a word.

THURSDAY, JUNE 16

It took us two days, but Ben made it all the way to the top of the mountain.

The weather held, and the sky was so clear that we could see all the way to the Atlantic Ocean.

But what I kept looking at was Ben. He was beyond exhausted. But he had made it. He was standing on the top of his mountain. And we didn't have to ask if it was worth the struggle. The satisfaction was all over his face.

"I want to remember this moment," I said to Luke.

I was expecting him to say something, but Luke just nodded.

"Are you okay?" I asked him.

"Yeah," he said. But his voice was wrong.

I moved to where I could see him better and then almost wished I hadn't. Luke's face was gray, and his forehead was tight with pain.

"What's wrong?" I said.

"I took Motrin earlier," he said. "I guess it's wearing off."

"Motrin for what?"

He didn't answer.

"Your head?"

He nodded.

I was struggling to stay calm. "Where does it hurt?"

"The whole right side."

My throat was closing up. "Okay, sit down."

He started to, but as he moved, he lost his balance, and I had to catch his arm before he fell.

"CAROLINE," I screamed. My voice echoed off the mountains, surrounding me with that one panicked word.

Caroline came scrambling across the rocky mountain top.

"What happened?" she said. She saw Luke, and the color drained out of her face.

"We have to get him off the mountain," I said.

"The train," Caroline said.

"We don't have tickets."

"I'll deal with that. Just get him over there."

And for the first time in my life, I watched Caroline flat-out run. I kept thinking that the train was going to be full. And had to keep reminding myself that if anyone could talk or bribe our way onto that train, it was Caroline. I had to stay focused. I had to get Luke to the station.

The others had reached us. I watched the realization hit each of their faces.

"Kyle, help me," I said.

He nodded and got his good arm around Luke.

"We're going to take him down on the train," I told them.

"We'll get the packs," Natalie said.

I knew they shouldn't. They aren't strong enough. But I couldn't tell them no. We all had to feel like we were doing something.

"Take trips," I said to Natalie. "And don't carry much."

"We won't," she said.

"I'm okay," Luke said. "I can walk."

But as soon as we let go of him, his balance wavered again. After that he let us help him.

We almost made it.

I could see the train and Caroline standing beside it. And my attention was so focused on that image, that I wasn't paying attention to where I put my feet. I took a step. A rock slid. And I went down.

It should have been a hard fall, but I managed to get a hand out to catch myself. For a second, I was relieved. Then I felt the sharp pain in my palm and the wet warmth gushing between my fingers.

I was bleeding.

If any of my friends had an open cut and my blood got into it, I could infect them.

Luke crouched down unsteadily beside me.

And I had to say, "You can't touch me."

My left hand was cradled against my chest, blood oozing out between my fingers. Blood that might as well be toxic venom.

"Let me see," Luke said.

I wanted to tell him no. But I didn't think he was going to move otherwise. And he had to move. He had to get off this mountain. So I slowly opened my fingers.

The cut was deeper than I thought. And it was bleeding—a lot.

Caroline came up to us then. "Come on," she panted. "They're holding the train."

She saw my hand and uttered a word that should have been smurfed.

The first aid kit was all the way back with our packs on the other side of the summit. And I was bleeding everywhere. Luke tried to untie the jacket from around his waist, but his hands were shaking too badly.

Caroline crouched down beside me. She used her jacket and Luke's to wrap up my hand. She couldn't use mine. It was covered in my blood.

"They only had two seats left," Caroline said as she carefully pulled me up to my feet. "The rest of us are on the next one."

Luke staggered, but made it to his feet. When he winced, I wanted to cry.

"They'll have an ambulance waiting at the bottom," Caroline said. "We'll meet you at the hospital."

I heard her words and I knew they were important. But all I could see was Luke's face. His color was getting worse.

Luke and I took the last two empty train seats. He slumped against the window. I sat down next to him.

"I'm okay," he said. Even though he knew I wouldn't believe him.

The blood had oozed out of our makeshift bandage and smeared onto my right hand. So now I couldn't even touch him.

The train started slowly chugging down the mountain and I started doing something I hadn't done in a decade, I prayed.

God and I are usually not on speaking terms. But today I was desperate enough to ask for help from anyone, even a deity I didn't trust.

Please don't let Luke die today. I'll do anything. *Just heal what's broken. Stop the bleeding. Let him live.*

The prayer felt hopeless. But it kept repeating through my mind, all the way down the mountain.

The ambulance was waiting at the bottom, just like Caroline had promised. And the EMTs came to meet us with blue gloved hands. I had to give them both of our medical statuses. I saw them flinch when I said HIV. But the EMT with 'Perkins' on his uniform covered it well.

They put Luke on the gurney and sat me next to Perkins in the back. He put on a second pair of gloves before peeling back the jackets. I felt him put pressure on the wound before he rebandaged my hand. I kept my eyes on Luke.

The monitor next to Luke's head was flashing out his pulse and blood pressure. They were both too high. I need-ed him to relax, to slow down the internal bleeding, to buy us more time. But telling him that his numbers were high would make him more stressed. We needed to talk about something else. I just didn't know what. Luke and I have spent almost a decade talking. But today I couldn't find words.

When we pulled up to the Emergency Room, there were two teams waiting.

"I'm coming with him," I said as the back doors of the ambulance opened.

"Not until they take care of your hand," Perkins said.

I wanted to scream and argue and throw something. But I knew he was right. They were never going to let me near another patient while I was actively bleeding. I had seen people physically removed from patient rooms before. I don't know where those visitors ended up. But they weren't with the people they loved.

My best chance of being able to be with Luke was to let them stitch up my hand.

I had to tell him goodbye.

I leaned down and kissed Luke's beautiful gray face. The lump in my throat was choking me. But I managed to say, "They have to sew up my hand. And then I'm coming right back to you. Just keep breathing until I get there."

Luke's cold hand touched my cheek. "I will, Aly," he said.

And I had to fight back the tears.

The paramedics unlocked his gurney and eased him out of the ambulance.

It was agony to watch them take him away. But I couldn't look away.

I was still staring at the doors Luke had disappeared through, when a voice said, "Miss."

I looked over at a man wearing a plastic trauma gown over his scrubs. He offered me a blue gloved hand down out of the ambulance. They had a wheelchair waiting for me. A chair I didn't want or need. But the sooner I cooperated, the sooner they could get the blood contained and I could get back to Luke. So I sat in the chair and let them take me back into the maze.

A nurse helped me change into a hospital gown. I knew I wouldn't get my clothes back. Things saturated with HIV infected blood are destroyed. I try not to think about what that says about me.

They had to call Massachusetts Department of Children and Families to get permission to treat me. Then they had to find the right person to complete the right form to give consent. I spent the time trying to figure out what was happening to Luke. He was eighteen and could give his own consent. That would speed things up at least. They would scan his head. I was sure of that. But I didn't know what would happen next. They couldn't fix what's broken. So would they let him die? Or would they try to do things to slow down the bleeding? I didn't know.

The medical staff finally came back into my cubicle with consent to treat me. But they still had to set everything up. It felt like they were moving in slow motion as they laid out their instruments and prepped my hand.

"Try to stay still," the ER doc said.

I tried. But it seemed to take forever for them to clean out the cut and numb my hand. I looked around, searching for anything to distract me, and made the mistake of looking up.

The lights hit my eyes, and a memory came crashing down over me.

I was seven years old, waking up on a bed, just like this one. The lights were so bright I tried to turn away, but my head couldn't move. Or my arms. Something was holding me down.

In my panic, my limbs flailed. Or at least they tried. But they couldn't move. I was trapped.

"It's all right," said a woman's voice. Her face appeared over mine, her head blocking out the blinding lights.

"My name is Dr. Daniels. You're in the hospital. We're taking care of you. Can you tell me your name?" She sounded so calm.

My voice was shaking. "Alyson."

"We're waiting for a report," Dr. Daniels told me. "If it's clear, we can take you off the backboard."

"I want my mom," I whispered.

"Was she in the car with you?"

I tried to nod, but my head couldn't move. The panic swelled up again.

"It's okay," Dr. Daniels said. "Was your mother in the car with you?"

"Yes."

"She's here," Dr. Daniels told me. "Another team is taking care of her."

"Dr. Daniels," a voice said from across the room. "The films are clear."

Dr. Daniels smiled. "That means we can get you out of this."

There were loud sounds of Velcro tearing and then they were helping me off the backboard. I could move enough to see the people in scrubs with plastic over the top. My arm was bloody, and my head was spinning.

"Can you tell me what hurts?" Dr. Daniels said as she shone a small light in my eyes.

"My head and my arm."

Cold metal touched my leg and I jumped. They were cutting away my tights. I tried to pull my leg away, but hands pinned me to the bed.

"It's okay," Dr. Daniels said. "We want to make sure we find all of your injuries so we can fix them. We'll get you a hospital gown with balloons."

I didn't want the hospital gown. I wanted my velvet dress and my tights and my mama. I tried to struggle. But a needle pricked my arm. Within a minute the world was growing hazy.

I was drifting away when I heard a man's voice say, "Dr. Daniels, you need to see this."

Then something pressed into my palm and my thoughts snapped back to the present. They were sewing up my hand.

Finally, the ER doc said, "Some gauze and a shot of antibiotics and we can get you out of here."

"I need to see Luke Harrison," I told him. "He was in the ambulance with me."

"Are you family?"

Technically, no. But Luke and Caroline are the closest thing I have to family.

So I said, "Yes."

The doc looked skeptical. But he said, "I'll ask."

I didn't know his name. He had probably told me, but I didn't remember.

My mind was hardly in that room. It was wherever Luke was.

I had known that this was coming. But I still wasn't ready to lose Luke. There are some things you're never ready to face. Somethings that are unbearable. But being away from him was worse. So after they left me in the room, I pulled on a second hospital gown and went looking for Luke.

I found him in a trauma bay, drinking a juice box.

A woman in scrubs was typing on the computer. She glanced over at me and said, "Can I help you?"

"She's with me," Luke said.

I walked across the room to him, still not completely convinced that he was there and talking to me. But when I got to the side of the bed and touched his face with my right hand, he was real.

"Your color is so much better," I said.

"Painkillers and steroids will do that," Luke said.

"How's your hand?"

"Fine." I was almost afraid to ask. "Larry?"

"Didn't burst," Luke said.

"You're sure?"

"Completely."

"I was so scared," I whispered.

Luke wrapped his arms around me and pulled me in close. "Yeah, me too."

It was a while before I was willing to let go so I could look at his face. "Then what happened?"

Luke looked almost amused. "I have an acute otitis media." He looked at the woman typing. "Did I say that right?"

"Perfectly," she said.

I stared at him. "An ear infection?"

Luke nodded.

The doctor spoke up from her rolling stool. "They can be extremely painful in adults and put enough pressure on the inner ear to impact balance."

"But in the ambulance, his pulse and blood pressure were so high."

"A natural response to pain," she said. "They're normal now."

I couldn't quite take this all in, and they weren't finished.

"There's something else," Luke said. "When they did the CT scan there was no sign of Larry."

I frowned. "They couldn't see it?"

"They're not sure it's still there."

I didn't understand. "What happened to it?"

"I have no idea," Luke said.

"Aneurysms can resolve on their own," the doctor told us. "It's just extremely rare for one the size of Luke's."

"It's gone?" I asked her.

"We would need more in-depth scans to be certain," she said. "But his CT was promising."

For more than a few seconds, I was overwhelmed. I heard the words and I understood them. But none of it felt real.

Caroline showed up with clean clothes for me. When we told her what we knew, she looked the way I felt, stunned and relieved and almost afraid to hope.

"The others are in the parking lot," she said.

But Luke shook his head. "We aren't telling anyone. Not even my parents. Not until we know for sure."

"How do we know?" I asked him.

"We make a trip to Dartmouth."

MONDAY, JUNE 20

Today, Luke, Caroline and I drove down to the Dartmouth-Hitchcock Medical Center. The three of us were quiet on the drive, but Caroline couldn't seem to stop moving. She hates hospitals. But she still insisted on making the trip with us.

"Whatever happens, we face it together," she said.

Luke told his family he was going for a check-up with his neurologist. We didn't say anything about a change. Luke was adamant about that. And our hope was so fragile.

Our first stop was the imaging center, where Luke would get a brain MRI.

"This will take a while," he said.

"How long?" Caroline asked him.

"An hour, maybe more."

"You have to be in that tube for an hour?" she said.

He nodded. "With a mask over my face to hold my head still."

"I feel claustrophobic just thinking about it," I said.

"You get used to it after a while."

But I couldn't get used to the idea, any more than I could get used to how empty the waiting room felt after Luke went back for his scan.

Once he was gone, Caroline said, "He's going to be fine."

I nodded, not sure which of us she was trying to convince.

It felt like days before Luke came back to the waiting room.

"Now what?" I asked him.

"Now we have to wait," he said.

"How long?" Caroline said.

"We'll see Dr. Martin in two hours. Do you want to get some lunch?"

"Sure," we both said, because it was something to do. But Caroline and I weren't hungry, and for the first time since I've known him, Luke wasn't either. The three of us just sat at an outside café pushing food around on our plates.

I hated the way Luke kept looking at me, as if he was trying to find the right words to say something that needed to be said. Before he could manage it, it was time for us to see Dr. Martin.

The neurologist was a thin man who reminded me more of a jazz musician than a doctor. He even tipped his chair back with a steady rhythm.

"I told you that you were one in a hundred million," Dr. Martin said. "And you certainly lived up to it."

"The aneurysm healed?" Luke said.

"Completely. And there are no other abnormalities. You have a clean bill of health."

Luke sat back hard in his chair. "I'm going to live."

Dr. Martin smiled at him. "With any luck, to a ripe old age."

This was really happening.

Luke said goodbye to Dr. Martin and his staff the way most people would say goodbye to old friends. An entire chapter of his life was finished. It was something I couldn't imagine.

On the way back to the car, Luke gave Caroline free rein to call the others while he called his parents. Luke spent most of five minutes convincing them that the aneurysm was gone. Then I could hear them celebrating through the phone.

All the way back to Trinity, Luke couldn't seem to stop smiling, and my mind couldn't stop spinning. Luke isn't terminal anymore. He's going to live.

This was so good. But there was still a panic growing inside me. Which didn't make any sense. I love Luke. Nothing's changed, except his life expectancy.

The truth hit me with enough force to throw me back into the seat.

I love Luke. But I only let myself fall in love with him because he was terminal.

He was safe, because he was dying.

But now this relationship could last as long as I live.

When we got to Luke's house, his parents came out to meet him. They were crying and wrapping their arms around him. They were so happy. They got their miracle.

I don't think the Harrisons would have minded if Caroline and I stayed, but we both sensed that this was a private moment. So, we left Luke to his family.

Caroline waited until the Harrisons' front door had closed before she turned to look at me. "It's unbelievable."

I nodded.

"One trip south and he got his whole life back. His future. Everything. Even sex."

My thoughts caught on that last word. "What?"

"I was waiting to tell you until after we found out for sure about his head. But I've been reading. And if Luke takes anti-virals, his chance of infection would be really low."

My throat was squeezing shut.

"You all can have a sex life someday."

She sounded so happy. I could barely breathe.

"Are you okay?" Caroline said.

"Yeah," I managed. "I'm just late." I hugged her. "I'll talk to you tomorrow."

Caroline frowned slightly as I let her go. But I smiled, with my best 'everything is great' expression, and then walked away. I waited until I was around a corner before I started to run.

I sprinted down the road toward the Millers'. But I couldn't outrun my thoughts. And I couldn't chase them away. They kept crashing into each other.

I can't do this. I can't sleep with Luke.

The one good thing about the HIV was that no one would ever want to have sex with me, ever. Why did Caroline have to find a damn loophole?

She's going to tell him what she found out. She's going to take the protection of HIV away from me.

I slowed down to a walk when I got to the Millers' and managed to look mostly calm as I passed through the downstairs. When I reached my room, I shut the door and leaned against it.

I had to fight down the panic.

I had to think.

I can put sex off until we're married, but that's not forever.

On our wedding night, he would expect it.

Another wave of fear erupted inside me, and I had to struggle to breathe.

I survived sex with Rick. I can survive it for Luke.

To be honest, I probably deserve it.

After everything I've done. After all the lies I've told, all the times I betrayed the people I love, I deserve to be hurt, and humiliated and powerless. But knowing that doesn't make it any less horrifying.

And what about Luke? If the idea of sex sends me into a panic, what's going to happen when we get there?

I don't know. I just know it's going to be bad. And Luke doesn't deserve that. He deserves someone who can share his whole life, who can be his lover, the mother of his children, all the things I can't be.

He deserves so much better than me.

Luke doesn't have to settle for the girl with HIV anymore. But he will. Because that's who he is. He promised he will always love me. And Luke keeps his promises. It's one of the things I usually love about him. But tonight, I hate it.

Because it means I have to be the one who ends this.

TUESDAY, JUNE 21

First thing this morning, while the sky was still gray, I got dressed in running clothes, pulled my hair back into a ponytail, and left the house. I didn't bother leaving a note for the Millers. I figured they wouldn't even wake up before I got back. It doesn't take that long to end a relationship.

All the way to the Harrisons', I tried not to think about the fact that this would be the last time I made the trip. Instead, I held onto the delusion that Luke and I would somehow stay friends. Because isn't that what people always tell themselves? I can rip someone's heart out and we'll still like being around each other.

Maybe if you tried dating and it fizzled out miserably. Maybe if when you kiss your friend, it felt like kissing your cousin. But not when you've been in love. Once you've fallen in love with someone, there's no going back to how things were before.

I got to Luke's house before I was ready to deal with any of this. But I doubted another hour would make it any easier. So I stood on the sidewalk and called him.

Luke sounded half asleep when he answered. But he still said, "Good morning, Beautiful."

The same tone that used to unravel me sent something hot and sharp twisting through my stomach.

"I'm outside," I said.

"Give me two minutes."

So I stood and I fidgeted until Luke opened the front door. He looked like he had just pulled on a shirt. But when he saw me, his smile reached all the way up to his eyes. It's what Caroline calls his Aly smile, because she says it only shows up when he's looking at me.

I pulled in a breath. But before I could say what I had come to say, Luke kissed me. Not a quick peck of hello, but a lips meeting mine with so much passion it took my breath away kind of kiss. When he pulled back, I was dazed, and he was smiling.

"I was going to come over later, but this is better," he said.

His warm fingers wrapped around my cold hand and he was leading me into his house, down the hall to the family room. We sat down on the couch, and the way he was looking at me, I didn't know how I was going to do this.

Finally, I managed, "You're going to live."

He smiled at me. "That's the rumor."

"You can have a future."

"That's a good thing. So why do you look like someone died?"

"You get to grow up and get married and have a family."

Luke nodded.

My words were shaking. "But I can't."

I saw the realization hit him.

"You can't have children?"

I shook my head. "The risk of infecting them is too high."

Luke was quiet for so long I half wished he would say something, just so we could move past this horrible silence.

But when he opened his mouth, I changed my mind. I didn't want him to say anything. But he did.

"Aly, I don't have any idea what I want to do for a living, or where I want to go to school. The one thing I'm sure of is that I want to spend my life with you. So if you can't have children, we'll adopt."

I stared at him.

Mama hadn't been willing to give up Rick for me. But Luke was willing to give up having a biological child, for me?

"I am not worth that much trouble," I whispered.

Luke framed my face with his hands and looked straight into my eyes. I was afraid he was going to see all of me, my shame, my brokenness. But if he did, he misunderstood it. Because he said, "You are worth any amount of trouble."

And something inside me came undone. I finally understood what people mean when they say they love someone so much it physically hurts.

Luke wrapped his arms around me and pulled me in so close that I could feel his heartbeat against my skin.

I was supposed to be ending this. But instead I was falling in love with him all over again.

WEDNESDAY, JUNE 22

I still haven't broken up with Luke or told my friends about Rick and the trial and the lies. I keep trying to catch my breath and find my balance. But life keeps hurtling forward, not caring that I'm not ready, that I don't know how to handle any of this.

Tonight, the Millers' babysitter cancelled at the last minute. So I offered to stay with the girls. I needed the distraction, and it was something I knew how to do. Mrs. Miller must have been desperate because she agreed to let me watch her children.

I made them dinner and then did the dishes while they watched a show about superhero princesses. Standing at the sink, with the sound of the TV blaring from the next room, I realized that this was where my mother was while Rick and I were in the living room.

I pushed that thought away. But my mom and Rick kept showing up. When Hattie called me "Mom". And when I saw my face above Gabby's in the bathroom mirror. I rushed the girls through brushing their teeth. Realizing too late that where we were going next would be worse. A little girl's bedroom.

Hattie and Gabby's room is a pale pink instead of yellow. And there are two beds instead of one. But still, it was too familiar. The dollhouse in the corner. The bookcase full of books. Stuffed animals and dolls spilling onto the floor.

"Aly."

I looked over at where Gabby was sitting in her bed.

"You need to check the closet," Gabby said. "For monsters."

"I can do that."

"There aren't any monsters in the closet," Hattie said from her bed.

But she also leaned to the side to watch as I opened the closet door.

Inside the girls' closet, I tried not to see the little clothes. But my mother was there like a ghost hanging my clothes in the closet the day we moved into Rick's house.

"As long as Rick loves us, everything will be fine."

I shut the closet door. "No monsters."

"You're sure?" Gabby said.

"Positive."

I ran my hand over the seam between the door and the frame. "And now I'm sealing the door shut with monster repellent."

Gabby watched, interested. Hattie pretended not to care.

I kissed the girls goodnight and left their room, shutting the door and then leaning against it. But I kept seeing the shape of their little bodies under the covers and the fear of monsters in Gabby's eyes.

When I was Gabby's age, and sitting in my bed in the dark, I didn't watch my closet. My eyes were on the door to the hall, watching and dreading the moment when Rick would come into my room.

Rick was the most terrifying thing in my life. But he was also the kindest.

It would have been so much easier if I could have just labeled him a monster. But I couldn't. Rick gave us a home and made Mama smile. He went with me to my first day of first grade. He met my teacher and took pictures with me at my desk. Just like a real daddy. In the daylight he called me his princess. In the dark, he called me a whore. I didn't know what that meant. Just that it was bad.

The same man who taught me to ride a bike, and celebrated every lost tooth, also locked my bedroom door and made me cry. But not always. Sometimes when he came into my room at night, he was gentle. Sometimes his touch felt almost good. Which just made it worse. It was more proof that there was something wrong with me. That I was dirty and bad. That I deserved the things he did to me.

But tonight, I thought about Gabby. If someone hurt her, I would never blame her. But it was different with me. I never told Rick no. I did what he told me to do. It was my fault. The sex, the HIV, the lies. All of it.

I made this mess. And now I have to be the one to deal with it.

THURSDAY, JUNE 23

Today was my last deposition. The next step is the trial. But first I had to get through my interview with the attorneys for the defense.

Rick told me what would happen if I ever told anyone about what happened between us. And today I had to say those words in front of a camera, for his people. They're going to let him see it.

Riding up in the elevator, I kept praying that time would slow down. But instead, the elevator seemed to speed up. The doors opened and there was Mr. Raleigh, waiting for me, like usual. But today, Ms. Snyder, my court appointed advocate, was standing beside him. She had never met me at the elevator before. I suspect she was trying to be comforting. But her presence had the opposite effect.

"Hello, Alyson," Mr. Raleigh said. "The defense team is set up in the conference room."

I couldn't quite manage words, so I nodded.

Ms. Snyder came up beside me. "Just stay calm and answer their questions truthfully."

But I wasn't calm. And it wasn't something I figured out how to achieve before we walked into the conference room.

Rick's lawyers introduced themselves as Ms. Stone and Mr. Barkley. They sat on the far side of the table. Ms. Snyder went to her usual corner. Mr. Raleigh took the chair beside me. The battle lines were drawn.

Mr. Barkley turned on the camera. Ms. Stone was the one who asked me to state my name for the record. Then the preliminaries were over.

Ms. Stone looked directly at me. "I have watched your earlier depositions, Miss Bennett. In them you allege that my client, Richard Wallace, sexually abused you. Is that correct?"

I had to work to keep my voice calm. "I don't allege."

"Mr. Wallace didn't abuse you?"

"No, he did. I mean alleged makes it sound like you don't believe me."

"And why should we believe you?"

"Because there was physical evidence. The DNA matched."

"There was a breech in the chain of possession, leading all of the physical evidence collected in the emergency room to be ruled inadmissible. Which means it can't be mentioned in any trial." Ms. Stone glanced at Mr. Raleigh sitting beside me. "The ADA should have told you that."

"I did," Mr. Raleigh said.

Ms. Stone's eyes came back to me. "So I will return to my original question. Do you allege that Mr. Wallace abused you?"

I hate the word allege, but I answered her question. "Yes."

"How many times?"

I faltered. "I don't know."

Ms. Stone raised an eyebrow. "You don't know?"

"It was almost every night, once it started."

"And when did it start?" Ms. Stone said.

I don't know the date. It was a few weeks after we moved into his house. June? July, maybe? I had to choose.

"The July that I was six."

"And when did the abuse allegedly stop?"

"December of the next year."

"So roughly seventeen months," Miss Stone said.

"Yes."

"Your mother was home during these assaults?"

I tasted blood and realized that I had bitten into the inside of my lower lip. "Yes."

"Where did the alleged abuse take place?"

"Most of it happened upstairs in my bedroom, when he was putting me to bed."

"And where was your mother?"

I swallowed around the lump in my throat. "Downstairs. Doing dishes. Watching TV."

He spent hours putting me to bed. But she never commented.

Ms. Stone's expression was incredulous. "Your mother was watching television while her boyfriend assaulted you in an upstairs bedroom?"

"Yes," I whispered.

"That doesn't seem likely, now does it?" Ms. Stone said.

My voice was shaking. "I don't know. I just know it's true."

Ms. Stone's face tightened. Her next questions came at me like bullets from an automatic weapon: sharp, fast and relentless. For hours she bombarded me, making me go over everything so many times I almost doubted myself.

"So you allege that Mr. Wallace assaulted you nearly every night for seventeen months and not only did you not tell anyone, not a single adult noticed, not your mother who lived in the house with you or your teachers who were trained to look for signs of child abuse. Is that correct?"

I knew how bad this sounded. But I also knew the truth. "Yes."

Ms. Stone flipped a page in her notes. "Do you have a boyfriend, Miss Bennett?"

"What?"

Ms. Stone looked up from her notes. "Do you have a boyfriend?"

"Yes."

"What is his name?"

"I don't understand what this has to do with anything."

"You don't need to understand," Ms. Stone said. "Just answer the question. What is your boyfriend's name?"

"Luke Harrison."

"And how long have you known Mr. Harrison?"

"Um, nine years."

"Would you describe your relationship as close?"

I shifted in my chair. "Yes."

"Do you love Mr. Harrison?"

"Yes."

"Do you trust him?"

"Yes."

"Do you talk to him about personal things?"

"Yes."

I didn't know where she was going until she said, "Have you told him about the alleged abuse?"

And my whole chest froze.

"Miss Bennett. Have you told your boyfriend about the alleged abuse?"

"No," I whispered.

Ms. Stone leaned forward in her chair. "You haven't told him about such a traumatic event in your life. Why is that?"

Because I lied about how I got HIV.

But I couldn't say that. If they knew I lied about that, why should anyone believe me about this?

I was bracing myself for her to press the point. But she didn't.

"You and your mother were in a car accident. How old were you when that happened?"

"Seven. Almost eight."

It was three weeks before my birthday.

"And did you suffer any head trauma during that accident?" Ms. Stone said.

"I had a bad headache afterwards."

"And during your time in the emergency room, what other injuries did they find?" Ms. Stone said.

"A deep cut on my arm, from the broken glass."

"And what else?"

I looked up at the ceiling tiles. "Sexual trauma."

It was what Dr. Daniels called it when she told my mother.

I was still groggy when Mama came through the swinging doors. She had a white bandage taped to her forehead. But she seemed all right, just worried about me.

Dr. Daniels had pulled her aside and spoken in a low voice. "Miss Bennett, your daughter has suffered severe sexual trauma."

"Th-that isn't possible."

"The evidence doesn't leave any room for doubt," Dr. Daniels said. "I have already contacted the police."

All of the color drained out of Mama's face. "I didn't know."

Dr. Daniels didn't comment.

Mama came over to me. She was shaky and pale, but she smiled at me. "I have to go home and get a bag for us. And then I'll be right back."

"Mama, don't go."

She squeezed my hand. "I'll be right back."

Ms. Stone's voice attacked me in the present. "So the

evidence of sexual abuse was found *after* you suffered a head injury in the accident. Is that correct?"

"Yes."

"Did you lose consciousness from this head injury?" Ms. Stone said.

"I guess so."

She nodded. "Did you suffer memory loss?"

"Just for part of the accident," I said.

I was telling her the truth, but Ms. Stone's face made it obvious that she didn't believe me.

"You don't actually remember who abused you, isn't that correct, Miss Bennet?"

"No. I remember."

"The police pressured you, and you named the first person you could think of, Richard Wallace."

"No."

Ms. Stone looked like a wolf circling her prey. "You haven't told your boyfriend that Mr. Wallace abused you, because he never did. Isn't that right?"

"No."

I looked to Mr. Raleigh to help me. But he just sat there as Ms. Stone's voice attacked me.

"You made up the accusations. Isn't that true, Miss Bennett?"

"No. Why would I go through all of this if it didn't happen?"

"Mr. Wallace is a wealthy man. You could be planning to sue him."

"I don't want his money. I want him to go to jail. You know what he did to me, and what he did to that other girl. How can you sit there and defend him?"

"I'm just doing my job, Miss Bennett."

I was out of my chair, my hands gripping the table. "He'll do it again. You know that. He gets off on hurting little girls."

I was done. Ms. Snyder was on her feet, but I didn't go near her.

I pulled the door open as Mr. Raleigh said, "Miss Bennett—"

But Ms. Stone's voice cut him off. "Let her go. We got what we needed."

I froze in the doorway. *We got what we needed.*

I had helped them.

Dear Olivia,

I saw Rick's lawyers today. It went badly.

When I left them, all I wanted to do was run away. I wanted to go somewhere where no one knows me. Somewhere where I wouldn't have to ever see Rick or step into a witness stand or tell my friends the truth.

I thought about Alaska. No one would think to look for me there. And I'm used to the cold. I told myself that Luke and Caroline would have each other. And eventually they would stop thinking about me. They would be fine.

But if I run, I would be abandoning you.

Without my testimony, they would need yours. They would make you face Rick and say those horrible words out loud.

I remember how terrifying that thought was as a little girl.

I can't leave you to face that alone.

I have to testify.

Which means I have to face my friends and tell them what I've done.

-Aly

SATURDAY, JUNE 25

I started with Caroline. I knew I'd want to back out. So I sent her a message that said, *I need to tell you something in person.*

She clearly knew this was serious, because she wrote back: *I'll meet you in the cupola.*

The cupola is a small glassed in room at the top of the hotel. When we were kids it was where we would sit and talk when we didn't want anyone to hear. The two times in my life that I've seen Caroline cry have both been in the cupola.

I spent the trip to the hotel trying to calm my nerves. But it didn't work. And before I was ready, I was running down the long tree-lined driveway to the Ballentine. I entered the hotel through a side door and started up the stairs, my steps growing slower with each floor I passed. But I still reached the fourth floor too soon. I opened one last door and slowly started my way up the steep staircase that leads to the small room at the very top of the hotel.

When I got to the top of the stairs, Caroline was already there, staring out at the mountains. Her whole body was tight.

And for one horrible second, I thought she already knew. But reason pushed in to tell me that wasn't likely. Not yet. Chances were, she was upset about something else.

"What's wrong?" I asked her.

She didn't look at me. "My father."

"What did he do now?"

"He had a son," she said. "With some woman in New York."

I walked closer. "You have a brother?"

Caroline finally turned to look at me. "I've had a brother, for three years. But my father didn't tell me until now."

I stared at her in disbelief.

"Exactly. He didn't tell me because he didn't want his new wife to find out he had cheated on her and use it against him in the divorce. But they signed the settlement yesterday, so he calls me today to tell me, oh, by the way, you have a sibling you knew nothing about."

Her face was tight and pale. "He is a lying, cheating bastard who doesn't care about anyone but himself."

I didn't know what to do but hug her. At first, she was stiff in my arms. But after a few seconds, she hugged me back. Caroline held onto me like she was drowning.

It was a long time before she pulled back and wiped her eyes. "But you aren't here about my disgusting father. What was it you wanted to talk about?"

"It can wait."

"No, tell me. I need to think about something else."

This was not the kind of distraction she needed. "I don't think that's a good idea."

Caroline's face was still hard, but her voice was tired. "I can't deal with anyone else keeping secrets right now. Just tell me, Aly."

There were alarm bells going off in my head. I couldn't think of a worse time to tell her. But she already knew I had something important to say, and if I didn't, she was going to get upset and this was going to be even more of a mess.

So I told her the truth. "I lied."

The pain on Caroline's face faded into confusion and anger. "You lied about what?"

My throat was closing up. This was a bad time.

"You lied about what?" Caroline's voice was getting sharper.

"About how I got HIV."

"You didn't get HIV from your birth mother?"

I shook my head.

"Then why did you say that?" Caroline said.

"I don't know. It-it just came out. And then you and Luke started passing on the story."

"Because we thought it was the truth."

"I know. But once you started telling people, I didn't know how to undo it."

Caroline's voice was rising. "You tell the truth."

"I've tried."

"Not very hard!" she screamed at me. "It's been a *decade*."

Caroline pulled back, breathing hard. "Do you even have HIV?"

I swallowed. "Yes."

Caroline met my eyes. "See, I don't know if that's true. Because you just told me you're a liar."

I've pictured this moment so many times, and I thought I knew what it would feel like. But I was wrong. It was so much worse than anything I had imagined. She was looking at me like I disgusted her.

"Get out," Caroline said.

I turned and stumbled down flights of stairs until I was out of the building and running across the back lawn. I didn't even know where I was going until I came in sight of the tool shed that Caroline's mom had let us turn into a clubhouse. I wrenched the door open and went inside. With the door shut, the only light in the room was what could filter through the layers of grime that had built up on the windows. The result was dim. But I was glad. I didn't want to see the cheerful pictures I had painted on these walls. It was all a lie. Just illusions to cover up the ugliness.

I sank down in the corner of that filthy floor, wrapping my arms around my bent knees, just trying to hold myself together.

It was hours later when I heard the door of the shed open and Luke's voice said, "Aly?"

I brushed my hands across my face, trying to wipe it clean of emotions. "Over here."

Luke came through the door. He saw me, but for once he didn't smile. He looked more concerned than happy.

"I called," he said. "But you didn't answer."

I looked around, but there was no sign of my phone. "I must have left it at the Millers'."

Luke nodded. "I talked to Caroline. She said you had a fight."

My heart seized up in my chest. "Did she tell you what it was about?"

"No, just that you were upset when you left."

After Mama and Caroline, I felt physically sick even thinking about saying the words. But I knew I needed to tell him. I was running out of time. "I have to tell you something."

Luke sat down next to me on the dirty floor. "Okay."

I took a breath and worked to form the words. I could hear them in my head, but when I opened my mouth there was no sound.

We sat there in silence for minutes before Luke said, "Maybe it would help if I tell you something first."

I knew it wouldn't. But I figured it would buy me a little time, so I nodded.

"I got subpoenaed yesterday," Luke said. "For a case against some guy named Richard Wallace."

I couldn't breathe.

"So I called the court in Boston. They told me that Richard Wallace is accused of a long list of things, including child rape."

There was no air.

Luke looked right at me. "I only know one person who lived in Boston as a child."

I wanted to run away. But I couldn't move.

This was my fault. I was stupid enough to say on video that I hadn't told my friends, including my boyfriend. Of course, Ms. Stone had noticed that. It was why she had asked me for the name of my boyfriend. So she could drag him into court.

"Did you know him?" Luke said.

I nodded. "He was my mom's boyfriend."

"When you were how old?"

"Six and seven."

Luke's breaths were uneven, and his voice was low. "Did he hurt you?"

I nodded. "That's how I got HIV."

I saw the rage overtake his face, saw it spread through his body, clenching his muscles and tightening his jaw until he looked more like stone than flesh. For the first time in my life, he terrified me.

Luke moved, and my arms came up to protect my head. I heard the impact crashing above me. Dust and wood fragments showered down.

When I peeked out, Luke was on his feet, and there

was a hole where his fist had broken through the shed wall.

His face was livid, until he saw mine.

Luke closed his eyes and forced himself to pull in deep breaths. His muscles were still tight as he crouched down in front of me. But his voice was quiet. "I'm sorry. I didn't mean to scare you."

I had to work to push words past the lump in my throat. "I lied to you."

Luke was frowning. "Aly, I'm not angry at you."

I didn't understand.

"It's the man who hurt you that I want to kill." Pain was mixing in with the rage on his face. "You were six years old."

It was agony to see him like that and know it was my fault. I couldn't look at his face. So I looked down and saw his hand.

"You're bleeding," I said.

"I'm fine."

But he wasn't. There was blood dripping from his right hand. He was hurt, because of me. That's not how love is supposed to work. I looked around the shed for anything I could use for a bandage. But there was nothing clean.

"We have to wrap your hand," I said.

"We don't."

I had to fix this.

"Here." Luke started to rip a strip of cloth off the bottom of his shirt.

"Don't ruin your shirt."

Luke tore it free anyway. "I don't care about the shirt."

His hand looked terrible. He needed to go home and clean off the cuts before they got infected. He needed a real bandage. He needed to get away from me.

But Luke didn't leave. He wrapped the strip of cloth around his bleeding knuckles, and then he slid in behind me, his legs framing mine, his arms wrapping around me. At first, I didn't know what to do. But he just held me. And eventually I pressed back into his chest. I didn't know what I was feeling. I just knew that Luke hadn't left me. And eventually, I found my voice again.

"I never meant to lie about how I got HIV. That first day in group when Marcus called it the sex disease, I panicked. I was so scared of what you all would think of me if you knew how I got HIV, so I lied. And then we became friends, and I didn't know how to undo it. You were my only friends, and I lied to you over and over again. I am so sorry."

"It hurts that you didn't trust us," Luke said. And I could hear the pain in those words. "But it's forgiven."

"It isn't forgivable."

"It's already done. When I was trying to make sense of the subpoena, I had to at least consider the possibility that Wallace hurt you and that was how you got HIV. I just didn't want it to be true."

My throat tightened. "Because it would mean I lied."

And that I'm filthy.

"Because it would mean you went through hell. And you've carried it around all this time. That I didn't figure it out."

"I didn't want you to figure it out."

"Why?" Luke said.

So many reasons. I told him one. "I thought you would leave."

His arms tightened, holding me closer. "I'm right here."

We sat there wrapped up in each other on the floor of an old tool shed for a long time.

It was Luke who eventually broke the silence. "Why is the trial now?"

"The DA decided that there wasn't enough evidence to get a conviction in my case. So they dropped the charges. Now Rick has been arrested for another girl and they want me to testify, to show a pattern."

Luke kissed my hair. "He's not going to win this time."

"The defense subpoenaed you because I never told you. They're going to claim I made the whole thing up."

"But they know he abused you," Luke said.

"It doesn't matter. All that matters is what the prosecution can prove."

I could hear Mr. Raleigh's voice and Ms. Stone's, both asking me questions I didn't want to ever answer, especially not in front of a room full of people. Especially not in front of Luke.

I looked down at Luke's arms still wrapped around me. "I need you to do something for me."

"Anything."

"I need you to stay out of the courtroom during my testimony."

"Why?"

I bit my lip. "Because I don't want you to hear that story."

"I won't punch anything," Luke said.

"It's not that."

"Then what?"

The tears were coming back. "I want you to still look at me like I'm good."

"That's not going to change." He sounded like he meant it.

"But you don't know what happened."

"Then maybe you should tell me."

My voice was shaking. "Please don't ask me to do that."

"Aly, look at me."

I didn't want to.

But I knew I owed him that much. So I slowly turned to look at him.

His eyes were as intense as I had ever seen them. But his voice was quiet. "If we're going to work, you're going to have to trust me."

He didn't know what he was asking. He couldn't. But apparently, I was too drained to be thinking rationally, because I said, "I'll tell you. But please, not here."

"Mom and Dad are at the lake. We can go there."

It was away from Caroline and bought me some time. So I nodded and let Luke help me to my feet.

We went to the Harrisons' house first. In the kitchen, Luke pulled out a medical kit the size of a toolbox.

"Your mother takes first aid seriously," I said.

"She has a reputation to keep up."

He pulled off his makeshift bandage, and we both looked at his hand. The cuts weren't bleeding anymore. But his skin was bloodied and bruising. Luke opened the kit and put the supplies he needed on the counter.

"Can you help me?" he said.

I took a step back. "You have open cuts."

"You aren't bleeding, Aly. You can touch my hand."

I looked up to study his face, but there was no concern there, no hidden fear.

"You aren't going to hurt me," he said.

He sounded sure. But it still took me a few seconds before I could make myself move closer to him. And my hands still felt unsteady as I opened a package of sterile gauze and doused it with hydrogen peroxide. I carefully took Luke's right hand in my left and started to clean the blood off his skin.

I hesitated when I reached the cuts across his knuckles. But then I carefully cleaned away the dried blood and applied the antibiotic ointment. He was going to have some nasty looking bruises, but nothing should get infected.

"Thank you," Luke said.

I didn't know if he should be thanking me. If it hadn't been for me, he wouldn't have hurt his hand in the first place. But at the same time, I was grateful for even a small chance to take care of him.

Luke threw some clothes in a bag and then we headed to the Millers'. I half hoped Mrs. Miller would tell me I couldn't go. But no one was home when we got to the house. I packed a bag, wrote the Millers a note, and climbed back into Luke's car.

We're headed south now. I keep telling myself it's going to be okay, that telling him won't be as bad as I think. But the truth is I don't know what's going to happen.

SUNDAY, JUNE 26

The Harrisons' lake house is small, just two bedrooms, a bathroom, and one room that serves as the living room, dining room and kitchen all in one. When we were kids, Luke, Caroline and I used to sleep in sleeping bags in the main room and wake up to the smell of blueberry pancakes. Mrs. Harrison always seemed happy to have me. But that was before Luke got subpoenaed because of me. And before the Harrisons found out I had lied. I didn't know what kind of reception I was going to have now.

But the Harrisons weren't surprised to see me, or hostile when Luke and I showed up at the lake yesterday.

"Aly, we're glad you're here," Mrs. Harrison said. "You're going to sleep in the boys' room. Luke can sleep on the couch."

I didn't want to kick Luke out of his own bed, but his mother's tone was final. So, I didn't argue.

I tried to help with dinner, failed to eat it, and finally went to bed. I thought I would lay awake for hours, but I was so exhausted I fell asleep almost immediately.

This morning, I woke up in a soft bed surrounded by covers that smelled faintly of Luke. And I felt safe—for the five seconds before I remembered what happened yesterday and why we were here.

Last night, Luke's parents were talking about taking the boat out today. So, I came downstairs wearing a t-shirt and shorts over my bathing suit. But Luke wasn't dressed for the water.

"I thought we could use the time to talk," he said.

It was why we were here. And why I wanted to go on the boat.

But Reverend and Mrs. Harrison left without us. From a window, I watched their small boat grow smaller as it sailed out onto the lake. I hated how quiet the house was now that it was just the two of us. It felt like the walls were closing in around me.

"Can we go outside?" I said.

"We can go wherever you want."

So I walked out onto the back deck. The fresh air was better. From the deck I could see the lake and an expanse of sky. I chose an Adirondack chair, and Luke dragged another around to face me. We sat there, our chairs so close that our knees were almost touching, while I tried to work up the courage to say the words.

I looked at Luke's t-shirt, studying the fabric as if I had never seen it before. I don't remember bringing my knees up. But then they were there, pressed up against my chest.

Slowly, I told him about meeting Rick, about moving into his house, about Rick blurring the lines and then breeching them completely. I couldn't bring myself to look at Luke's face, so I watched his hands. More than once, they looked ready to hit something. But Luke didn't say anything. He just listened.

When I got to Rick's birthday, I wanted to stop. I wanted this to be over. To not have to tell him what happened next. But if I stopped here, I didn't know if I would ever tell him the rest.

"Whatever it is, you can tell me," Luke said.

I kept seeing the disgust on Mama's face when I tried to tell her. The thought of that same look taking over Luke's face was unbearable. But I didn't think I could go back to living in dread either. Luke was right. If this was going to work, I was going to have to trust him, even with the horrible parts.

I took a deep breath and tried to calm down, but my hands wouldn't stop shaking. Luke reached over to hold my hand. And finally, I said the words.

"I took off my clothes. I lay down on the bed. I did everything he told me to do." I felt sick. But I had to finish this. "Sometimes he hurt me. Sometimes he didn't. Sometimes his touch felt almost good."

Shame was drowning me. And silence stretched out between us. Luke couldn't even talk to me. He was too disgusted. I knew that.

When his hand touched my cheek, I jumped.

"Aly, look at me."

I didn't want to look at him ever again.

But he said, "Please." Just like he had the night he first told me he loved me.

It's always the "please" that undoes me. I slowly lifted my eyes and looked at him.

"It wasn't your fault," Luke said.

I shook my head. He didn't understand.

"My body—"

"Did exactly what it's designed to do. Exactly what he knew it would do." Luke was looking straight into my eyes. "He set you up, from the beginning. He knew how to manipulate you into doing what he wanted, how to make you feel dirty and guilty so you would keep the secret. But you have nothing to be ashamed of."

"I gave in," I whispered.

Luke nodded. "I know. And I'm glad. If you hadn't it could have been worse. And I can't stand the idea of Wallace hurting you any more than he already did."

I stared at Luke.

He has never been good at masks. He was right. His love for me had been all over his face. Caroline had seen it. Even Kyle had seen it. I had only missed it because I was so convinced that no one could ever love me that way. But Luke's face doesn't lie.

And today, as I looked at him, there was no revulsion in his expression. There was love and rage and heart break. But no disgust when he looked at me.

His right hand closed around mine. "None of it was your fault. Rick raped you."

I've never used that word. It's too violent. Too one-sided.

But I knew that Luke was right.

I loved Rick. I trusted him. And he raped me.

Sobs were building up in my chest, tears sliding down my cheeks. I don't remember moving, but I felt Luke's shirt against my cheek and his arms wrapping around me. And finally, I let myself cry.

I cried for the six-and-seven-year-old little girl who had been trapped in a nightmare and for the eight-year-old who was too terrified to tell her friends the truth. I cried for the girl who knew that she was too dirty to ever be loved, for the girl who was drowning in shame.

I cried until there was nothing left inside of me.

Dried tears coated my skin and an ache still lingered in my chest. I was exhausted and empty, and somehow a little freer.

Luke hugged me tighter and then stood up, taking my hand. "Come on."

I let him lead me off the back deck and around to the outside shower. It's just a shower head jutting out from the side of the house with a sandy drain beneath it. A makeshift shelf held bottles of shampoo and body wash.

Luke reached over to turn on the shower. This seemed slightly insane, but I was too tired to argue. And once I stepped into the shower and felt the warm water hit my face, I was able to pull in a deep breath.

Luke took a bottle of body wash off the shelf. The water was plastering his shirt to his back, but he didn't seem to care. He just put a little soap on his fingers and reached toward me. I closed my eyes and just felt the gentleness of his touch against my skin. Slowly, methodically Luke washed the dried tears from my cheeks and my throat.

When he was done, he stepped back, and let the water rinse it all away.

Shame feeds on secrets. But Luke knew. And he was still here. He knew everything, and he still loved me. Was willing to get soaked for me. And as I realized that, I felt shame lose its grip.

"I didn't think it was possible for someone to know all of this and still love me," I said.

Luke stroked my wet cheek. "You are so brilliant about so many things. But you have a lot to learn about love."

He was right. But in that moment, I didn't care. I leaned forward and felt his arms wrap around me. We were both soaked, but we just stayed there, wrapped up in each other.

When the water finally turned cold, Luke turned off the shower and took my hand. We walked back toward the house together. It was as we were rounding the corner, that we heard a car coming down the gravel driveway.

"Who's here?" I asked

"I could only guess."

We turned the corner and saw Caroline getting out of her car.

My steps slowed. "You called her?"

"I just told her where we were."

"Did you tell her—"

"No."

Caroline started walking straight toward me. There was no smile on her lips, no devilish glint in her eyes. Her face was as serious as I had ever seen it. And she was walking toward me with so much force I wanted to step back. But I didn't. I just stood there, ready for whatever she was going to throw at me.

Caroline didn't yell at me or slap me. She threw her arms around me and hugged me, soaking wet clothes and all. I didn't know what to do but hug her back.

"I'm sorry," I told her again.

"I wasn't thinking," she said. "When I finally stopped acting like a complete ass, I remembered that this is *you*. And if you lied there was a reason. I just didn't like any of the options I came up with."

"You aren't going to like the truth either," I said.

"I'll live." Caroline took in our soaked clothes and Luke's hand. "You really need to start talking."

"Dry clothes first," I said.

We walked into the house, and I went into the boys' room to change. When I got back, I found Caroline sitting on the couch.

"Luke went to the store," she said.

It was just the two of us in the house. But I felt different than this morning. I didn't want to tell this story again. But the shame wasn't strangling me the way it had a few hours earlier. I sat down next to Caroline. And for the second time today, I told the story of what happened after Mama and I moved in with Rick. I gave her the short version. But it was still enough to send her spewing off curses I had never heard before.

I loved her for that. Because we get angry at the idea of someone hurting the people we love.

"Where was your mom in all this?" Caroline said when she had finally run out of expletives.

"Downstairs." The lump was back, trying to suffocate me. But I had done this once, so I knew I could do it again. "I told her that Rick was hurting me. I even tried to tell her how. But she didn't believe me." I could taste soap, smell burned eggs, hear Mama's footsteps walking away. "She didn't make it stop."

Caroline said something that should have been smurfed.

"Mama and I were in a car accident just before I turned eight. And while I was in the ER, they found evidence of the rapes. The doc told Mama. She got all pale and shaky and told me she was going to go home and get a bag for us. But she never came back."

I've known she left me. But saying things out loud makes them real. And God, it hurt.

Caroline wrapped her arms around me. Her grip was so tight I thought she might crack one of my ribs. But I didn't want her to let go.

For minutes she just held onto me.

When she finally pulled back, Caroline said, "You told your mom what was happening, and she did nothing. That makes her guilty as hell, and she knew it. Her leaving you at the hospital had nothing to do with you, and everything to do with her."

That helped, a little. The fact that she was still there helped even more.

"We need ice cream," Caroline said.

Luke came through the door with the words, "I have six kinds."

"He may be worth keeping around," Caroline said.

And I hadn't even told her about the shower yet.

When Luke's parents got back from their boat trip, they didn't seem surprised to see Caroline. I guess we do tend to end up together when things go wrong. They fed us dinner and went to their room, leaving the three of us to take care of each other.

We stayed up late, talking about Rick, and lots of other things. Which was a relief. For so long, my dread about telling them came in two levels. First, that they would hate me. Second, if they didn't hate me, I worried that they wouldn't be able to look at me without thinking about that. So a wandering conversation about everything was perfect.

Luke fell asleep first, sprawled across one of the couches. I don't think he's slept much in the last few days. Caroline and I moved over to the other couch and sat with our feet tucked under us, the way we have a thousand times before.

"So Rick is why you've never wanted to date anyone," Caroline said.

I nodded. "Even with Luke, it gets complicated."

"How?"

"I know he's not Rick. But it gets confused. Luke kissed me once in the mural room and slid his fingers into my hair, and suddenly I was thrown back into a memory. It was like it was happening all over again."

"Did you tell him?"

I shook my head. "I didn't want to hurt him."

"He would want to know," Caroline said. "And you *need* him to know."

"I wanted to handle this myself."

"I know," she said. "But there are some things we can't do on our own. We're wounded in relationships, and we heal in relationships."

"Which therapist said that?"

"The second one, with the puppets."

The woman may have been slightly disturbing, but she had a point.

"Let Luke help you through this," Caroline said.

I looked at the rocks that make up the fireplace, each piece fitting with the one beside it. "I don't know if I want to get through this."

"Meaning what?"

I looked back at her. "Meaning that the idea of sex horrifies me."

"The thought of a repeat of Rick horrifies you," Caroline said. "But that wasn't sex. That was a sick imitation."

She was right. Rick had taken something that should have been a gift in my life and twisted it into a horrific weapon. But now that's what fills my head.

"I can't even think about sex without panicking," I told her.

"It won't always be like that."

"How do you know?"

"Because I know you."

"Even after today?"

"Even better after today," Caroline said. "I've always known you were strong and brave. But I have a whole new appreciation now."

I shook my head. "I'm not."

"If you weren't strong, you wouldn't have survived. And if you weren't brave, you never could have risked loving someone again. Not after what had happened to you." Caroline's face sharpened. "And that bastard has stolen enough from you. He doesn't get to steal your future too."

I've never let myself think about the future. But tonight, after Caroline and I had gone to bed, I let my imagination wander.

The scene grew slowly. It was early in the morning. My head rested on Luke's bare chest. His arm was wrapped around me, holding me close. In the distance we could hear a baby cry.

Luke kissed my hair. "I'll get her."

He pulled on a shirt as he left the room. He was back a minute later with a baby in his arms. He laid our daughter in the bed between us, and she smiled at me, waving her little arms. I looked from Luke to our child, and I was completely overwhelmed by love.

I love that idea and that there's a chance it could happen.

I just don't know how to get from here to there.

MONDAY, JUNE 27

Luke likes watching the sun rise over the lake. So when I woke up this morning and found his couch empty, I pulled on a sweatshirt and opened the doors that led onto the deck. I found him sitting in an Adirondack chair, staring off at where a smudge of light had broken through the horizon.

When he saw me, he smiled. "Morning."

"Morning."

I crossed the deck to kiss him gently before I slid into the Adirondack chair beside his.

For a few minutes, we just sat in the quiet of the morning, watching the light slowly grow.

I knew that if I was really going to let Luke help me through this, there was something I needed him to understand. I just wasn't sure how to explain it. The best I could come up with was a movie reference.

"Do you remember the movie where all of the girl's emotions were different characters who lived inside her head?"

"It's kind of hard to forget," Luke said. They made us watch it every year in Kids' Group.

"There was Sadness, and Anger and Fear and Disgust—"

"And Joy," Luke said.

"Right." *Joy.* I pulled in a breath. "I feel like I have an extra emotion. Dread."

If Luke thought I had lost my mind, it didn't show on his face. So I kept talking.

"She's a six-year-old little girl who's still trapped in that house."

Luke' reached over to hold my hand.

"Caroline thinks I can marry you someday and have everything that comes with that."

"Including sex," Luke said.

Heat rushed into my cheeks, but I nodded. "And I want all of that. But every time I seriously think about it, that one piece panics."

"That was the part that freaked out in the mural room," he said.

I nodded again. "You slid your fingers into my hair, and it set off a flashback."

"Aly, I'm sorry."

"You didn't know. I didn't either. Just like the night on the side of Mount Washington."

Luke's face shifted, thinking back.

"I looked back and saw a man's shadow framed by two trees. And it looked like Rick standing in my doorway. In my head, I was back in that room, and Rick was coming to hurt me. But then it was you, asking if I was cold. You gave me your sweatshirt."

"And that helped?"

I nodded.

There are times I feel like I'm walking through a minefield, never knowing when something is going to blow up in my face. But I know about a few land mines now, and I wondered.

"Will you do something for me?" I asked.

"Anything," he said.

"That's a dangerous promise."

"There aren't any bodies to move."

I smiled at him.

"What do you need me to do?" he said.

"Slide your fingers into my hair."

Luke shifted back in his chair. "You just said that went badly."

"I know. But I don't know of another way to convince that one terrified part that it's different when you do it."

Luke still looked concerned about this plan. But when I stood up, he came with me. We were barely a foot apart.

"You're sure?" Luke said.

I nodded.

So Luke reached out his hand and stroked the side of my head. My breaths were coming faster, but I didn't move. Luke slid his fingers into my hair, and the memory came crashing down around me.

I gasped, and Luke started to pull away. But my words came out in a rush. "Don't leave."

"I'm right here."

I could feel Rick's hand twisting through my hair, feel the tears on my cheeks and the desperation in my chest. But I knew it wasn't happening again. It was a memory. I was at the lake with Luke.

"I'm safe."

"Completely," Luke said.

I pulled in a deep, shaky breath. I wasn't a six-year-old child. I wasn't trapped in Rick's house. I didn't have to do anything out of guilt or fear. I was standing on the deck with Luke, because it was where I wanted to be.

The memories of Rick were still there, but they were fading. I felt the strength of Luke's hand, the tenderness of his touch, the intensity of the love in his eyes. And I was overwhelmed. I reached up and kissed him.

I had kissed Luke before. But never like this. Never without secrets or shame. Never with complete abandon.

And we stood on the deck, lost in the wonder of that kiss, as the sun rose over the water.

TUESDAY, JUNE 28

Driving into Trinity today was surreal. Everything looked the same but felt different. My friendships have changed. I've changed. But the trial is still there, waiting for me. Only now the countdown is in days—seven days until I have to face Rick.

When we got back to the Harrisons' house, Mrs. Reese was waiting for us.

"Mom," Caroline said. "What are you doing here?"

"We thought it was time we all had a talk," Mrs. Reese said.

I glanced at my friends. But they looked as surprised as I felt. The three parents sat down on one side of the Harrisons' living room. Luke, Caroline and I sat on the other. All five of them were watching me.

"Normally, we would say it was your parents' place to ask this question," Mrs. Harrison said. "But your parents aren't here."

"And your foster parents aren't winning any awards," Mrs. Reese added.

Luke's dad looked right at me with eyes that were so much like his son's, and said, "Aly, is there something you need to tell us?"

Need? Probably. Want? No. I don't want anyone else to know about this.

But Luke has been subpoenaed. He has to go to the trial. And chances are at least one of his parents will go with him. They're going to find out. And I needed to be the one to tell them.

"I have to testify in a trial," I told them. "Against the man who abused me when I was young. The one who gave me HIV."

Luke's parents would have been good poker players. They didn't flinch. Mrs. Reese's face took on a look of rage that was worthy of her daughter.

"The same trial Luke was subpoenaed to testify in," Mrs. Harrison said.

"Yes. They're going to use the fact that I didn't tell him about the abuse to try and make it look like I made the whole thing up."

"They know how often children keep this a secret," Reverend Harrison said. "They're just trying to rattle you."

It's working.

"Have you talked to a lawyer?" Mrs. Harrison said.

"Just Mr. Raleigh, the prosecutor."

"His job is to get a conviction. You aren't his first concern," Mrs. Harrison said.

"I'll call Dan Richards," Reverend Harrison said.

"We'll need rooms in Boston," Mrs. Reese said. "I'll take care of it."

Lawyers and hotel rooms cost money. Money I don't have.

"We'll cover the cost," Mrs. Harrison said as if she was reading my thoughts. And Mrs. Reese nodded.

I tried to protest, but Mrs. Reese leaned forward and said, "You're family, Aly."

And something caught in my throat.

"Thank you," I managed.

"What else do you need?" Reverend Harrison said.

For Rick to die suddenly sometime in the next week so I wouldn't have to do this. Barring that, there was one more thing that would help. But I'm terrible at asking for things. And they were already doing so much.

"What is it?" Caroline said.

"Can I have the wall?" I asked Mrs. Reese.

"What wall?" Mrs. Reese said.

"The ruined wall in the mural room. The one you want to tear down. I know it would cost less to tear it out and start over and that trying to keep it could delay opening the wing. But I think I can save at least part of the painting."

Everyone in the room was looking at Caroline's mother, waiting for her answer.

"Fine," Mrs. Reese said. "You can have until the end of July."

"It won't take that long," I promised.

"It isn't your only obligation," Mrs. Reese said.

It's just the only one I want to think about.

WEDNESDAY, JUNE 29

"They're here," Caroline said.

"I changed my mind," I told her.

"Too late," she said and left the room.

"I could write them letters."

"You know it's better face to face," Luke said.

In that moment, I wasn't sure. But then Caroline was walking back into the room with Ben, Kyle and Natalie following behind her. Caroline came to stand next to me and Luke. The other three turned, taking in the finished mural and the paint supplies laid out in front of the ruined section of wall.

"Aly, this is amazing," Natalie said. She looked back at me, her eyes shining. "You even included Anne of Green Gables. I adore her."

"I know," I said. It's why she made the list.

Ben's hand rested on the image of an enormous lion with deep, wise eyes. Kyle was grinning at Max from *Where the Wild Things Are.*

"Why didn't you tell us you were almost done?" Natalie said.

"There's a lot I haven't told you."

Ben and Kyle both turned to look at me. They were all watching me now.

"Maybe we should sit down," I said.

I told them an abbreviated version of the story, skipping over the worst of the details, and finished with, "Rick's going on trial next week for attacking another girl. And I'm going to testify."

Silence stretched out around us.

"They aren't saying anything," I whispered.

"Give them a minute," Luke said. "It's a lot to take in."

Their faces were struggling. I wished they would say something.

But it was Caroline's voice that broke the silence. "Show of hands. Who thinks Rick Wallace should die a slow and horrible death?"

Caroline's hand was already in the air. Luke joined her, followed a second later by Ben, Natalie and Kyle.

"Who's hurt that Aly lied to us, but understands why she did it?"

Natalie's hand was up almost as quickly as Luke and Caroline's. Ben's followed. Kyle's face was still struggling, but as he looked at me, his hand rose slowly into the air.

"Who still loves her?"

One by one, every hand in the room rose. Even Kyle's.

Tears started sliding down my cheeks.

Natalie was the first to stand up. But Ben reached me before she did. The two of them wrapped their arms around me, and I closed my eyes. I felt Luke and Caroline join the massive hug. And a minute later a prosthetic arm touched my shoulder.

I wasn't the only one who cried.

FRIDAY, JULY 1

When I was in fourth grade, there was a split in the sidewalk outside our school. The gash was big enough that it was considered a hazard. So a man came and filled it up with cement. But he rushed the job and the cement dried in an uneven mound rather than a smooth line. Eventually, another team had to come out with a jackhammer, tear out the patch, and refill the gap.

That's how I feel. Like as a little girl I had this gaping wound I didn't know how to deal with. So I filled it in with cement. That worked, in a way. No one could see how broken I was. And I was able to push down most of the pain. But the wound never healed. It festered.

Now I've torn away the patch. And there's incredible relief in that. But that choice also exposed the gash.

Most of the time, I'm fine. But then suddenly, out of nowhere, the pain comes back. And with nothing to dull it, I'm completely overwhelmed.

Painting has helped.

I've thrown myself back into the mural room. Only now, instead of creating, I'm restoring. Or at least, that's the idea.

Once I had gotten rid of as much of the soot as I could, I tried to paint, but quickly discovered that my usual techniques weren't going to work. The wall was too delicate. I had to work slowly, in small, incremental steps. There were moments when I had made real progress, only to have a whole section flake off and set me back hours. But I took a deep breath and started again.

This was turning out to be more complicated than I had expected. Because even when my technique was working, I still struggled to know what to paint. I wanted to be true to the original. But there were times it was difficult to tell what had originally been there. The colors were too faded, and whole sections of mural were gone. I realized I couldn't make this the exact painting that it was. And I couldn't undo what had happened to it. But I could bring that little girl back to life. The fire might have changed her. But it hadn't destroyed her. And with a little help and a little time, she could be as beautiful and alive as she had ever been. Maybe, even more beautiful.

I don't know what surrounded her in the original painting. But I'm making her a meadow full of flowers. I debated what to do with her sky, but eventually decided on beams of sunlight breaking through a sea of dark clouds.

Today, I was working on those strands of light when Caroline came into the mural room, pushing an enormous wheeled laundry cart.

"Are you trying to smuggle Annie out of the orphanage?" I asked her.

"Later," Caroline said. "First I have to fold a billion white towels."

She dragged in a comfortable chair and sat down with her mountain of towels.

Caroline spread a towel across her lap. "Are we talking or not talking?"

"Are you capable of not talking?"

"I am if that's what you need."

I gave her a skeptical look.

"Folding towels has a very calming effect," Caroline said. "Soon people are going to give up yoga and raking sand and just fold towels to reach inner peace."

"You could lead workshops. Turn the Ballentine into the premier towel-folding retreat."

Caroline's face lit up with possibilities. "People would come from all over the world to fold towels. We could cut staff and increase profits."

"That doesn't sound very Zen."

"My mother's genes broke through my inner peace," Caroline said.

"Maybe you should practice silent meditative towel-folding."

"I can do that."

And she did. Which led me to think there might actually be something to the Zen art of towel-folding.

"Okay, I'm done being Zen," Caroline said a few hours later.

"You've reached inner peace?"

"In an, 'I don't get paid after four o'clock' kind of way," Caroline said. "But I get another chance tomorrow."

"It's a long journey," I said.

For both of us.

SUNDAY, JULY 3

The trial starts in two days. I barely slept last night. I lay awake for hours trying to put my memories into some kind of logical order, trying to make sense of things that don't make sense.

This morning I didn't want to go anywhere or see anyone. But Mrs. Miller didn't care how bad my night had been. She expected me to go to church and smile like everything is fine. I don't know what she's going to tell people when I leave tomorrow. Maybe she'll say I'm somewhere with the Harrisons or the Reeses. Whatever it is, it won't be the truth. Because Mrs. Miller doesn't ever want to talk about things that are uncomfortable. She thinks we would all be better off if we ignored unpleasant topics.

Apparently, Luke's dad doesn't agree. Because this morning in church, Reverend Harrison ignored the readings listed in the bulletin and didn't go near the pulpit. Instead, he walked down the steps that lead from the altar to the nave and stood in front of the first pew.

"This morning, I would like to tell you a story found in the Old Testament Book of Esther. It's the story of a selfish and powerful king who decided he wanted a new queen.

"So, the king sent his soldiers out to collect young girls who had never slept with a man. The girls weren't given a choice. They were simply taken, from their homes, their families, the lives they knew, and imprisoned in the king's palace. One of those girls was named Esther.

"The night came when it was Esther's turn to be sacrificed to the king's appetites. He stole more than her innocence that night. He took her power and her voice. And the next day he married her, sentencing her to spend the rest of her life trapped inside his palace.

"One day after she was married, Esther's cousin Mordecai sent her a message, telling her there was a plot to kill all of the Jews. Mordecai asked Esther to go before the king and plead for the lives of her people. He told her, 'Perhaps you have been placed in your position for such a time as this.'

"Now, Esther was afraid. Not because she was weak. But because she knew the law. To go before the king without his summons was punishable by death. To do what Mordecai asked, she would be defying the king's rules and risking the wrath of the man who could destroy her. To make matters worse, Esther had a secret. No one in the palace knew that she was a Jew.

"Fear told Esther to protect her secret and her life, to

avoid the king's wrath at all costs. But there were innocent lives at stake. And no one else could take her place. So despite her fears, Esther agreed to go before the king. As she prepared to do what seemed unthinkable, Esther made one request. She asked her community to pray for her for three days.

"On the third day, Esther walked the long corridor that led to the throne room. She was terrified. But she found courage in the fact that she wasn't alone. Her entire community was standing with her.

"And as her feet carried her closer and closer to the king's throne room, she realized something else. Something vitally important. She was strong enough to tell the truth."

Reverend Harrison looked right at me. "Esther's innocence may have been stolen from her at a young age. She may have been isolated in her heartache and burdened with her secrets. But out of her experiences grew an opportunity, not to change the past, but to redeem it. To bring beauty out of ashes. To see justice served.

"And so, with her head held high, Esther walked through the enormous doors and faced the king."

"Did she win?" asked a boy from the middle of the church.

His mother hushed him, but Reverend Harrison smiled.

"Yes, Charlie," he said. "It wasn't quick or easy. But in the end, she won."

TUESDAY, JULY 5

The trial started today. I threw up twice before we ever left the hotel room. When I opened the bathroom door, Caroline unzipped her makeup bag. With a little foundation and blush, she made me look almost human again.

The Harrisons were waiting for us in the hall. Luke was wearing his funeral suit. I tried not to think too much about that.

No one ate much of the complimentary breakfast served in the lobby. Long before I was ready, it was time to drive to the courthouse.

Mr. Raleigh was waiting for us in the hallway outside courtroom three. "Good morning," he said.

I introduced my entourage, who all shook his hand.

"Is the girl here?" I asked him.

"No," Mr. Raleigh said.

Part of me was glad she wasn't there. That she didn't have to listen to what was going to be said in that room. But at the same time, I wanted to see her.

"Are we starting with jury selection?" Reverend Harrison asked.

"No," Mr. Raleigh said. "Mr. Wallace waived his right to a trial by jury. The verdict will be decided by Judge Baxter."

I was a little relieved that there will be fewer people in that room watching me. But I still had to ask, "Why would he do that?"

"Juries tend to be more driven by emotion, especially in cases involving children," Mr. Raleigh said. "Judges are more likely to decide the case based on its merits."

"So a jury would have helped us," I said to no one in particular.

"Probably," Mr. Raleigh said. "But Judge Baxter is fair. He will weigh all of the evidence."

Except I didn't have physical evidence. It was all thrown out.

"We'll have the opening statements first," Mr. Raleigh said. "Then we'll begin with the first witness. Alyson, you'll be fourth."

I didn't know if I should be happy about that or not.

Luke and I aren't allowed in the courtroom until it's our turn to testify. But Mrs. Reese went in to serve as our court correspondent.

When Mr. Raleigh opened the door and held it for Mrs. Reese, I got a good look at the courtroom. It looks almost the way I had pictured it, except there were no windows. Otherwise, it looked like the ones from TV, rows of seats for spectators, then the bar. The judge's raised bench and the jury box were empty. But the defense table wasn't. I saw Miss Stone and her lackey and beside them, Richard Wallace.

Even from behind I knew him, the shape of his shoulders, the cut of his suit.

"That's him?" Luke and Caroline said at almost exactly the same time.

I nodded.

I could feel the rage they were directing at the back of Rick's head. But I didn't feel angry. Maybe I should have. But I didn't. I felt cold.

The court room doors swung shut, blocking Rick from sight. But I still knew he was there on the other side of the wall. And I kept hearing his voice whispering to me.

Luke and Caroline and Luke's parents spent the entire morning trying to distract me. We walked all of the halls of the courthouse, taking note of which vending machines offered which items and which floor had the cleanest restrooms.

At lunch, Mrs. Reese gave us the recap of the morning. "Opening statements took about half an hour. The prosecutor said he did it; the defense team said he didn't. Then Raleigh called his first witness, a woman whose mother had dated Wallace when she was a little girl. He touched her. She told her mother. They moved out. Raleigh questioned her for forty-five minutes."

Mrs. Reese started to eat as if she was finished with her account.

The trial started at nine. They broke for lunch at twelve. That left an hour and forty-five minutes unaccounted for.

"So what did they do for the rest of the time?" I asked her.

And for the first time in my life, I saw Caroline's mother look uncomfortable. "Cross-examination."

And it had been bad. I could see that much on Mrs. Reese's face.

"Ms. Stone tore her testimony apart," I said quietly.

"We don't know that," Reverend Harrison said.

But I was looking at Mrs. Reese's face and I knew I was right, even before she nodded.

After lunch, Mrs. Reese went back into the courtroom to watch Ms. Stone continue to brutalize the prosecution's first witness. The rest of us stayed in the hall, the four of them giving me reassuring looks and then exchanging concerned glances.

Around three o'clock, the doors of the courtroom opened, and half a dozen people came out, including Mrs. Reese.

"We're taking a fifteen-minute recess before Mr. Raleigh calls his second witness," Mrs. Reese told us.

I did the math. Ms. Stone had spent almost four hours cross-examining a witness who said Rick had only gotten as far as touching her. At that rate, she was going to spend days on me.

FRIDAY, JULY 8

Today was trial day four.

The morning was agonizing. Ms. Stone was cross-examining the prosecution's third witness. When she finished, it would be my turn to take the stand. I almost wished that time would speed up so I could get this over with. Almost.

Minutes before twelve, the courtroom doors opened, and a stream of people came out. I was looking for Mrs. Reese, but I saw another woman. I had seen her a few times, coming in and out of the courtroom. But today, she looked at something on my side of the hall, and I saw her face. Her hair was shorter, her clothes more sophisticated. But her face was still the same, only now in more expensive makeup.

My mother had just walked out of the courtroom.

She disappeared with the crowd headed downstairs to find lunch.

"What do you want?" Caroline said.

I didn't look at her. "What?"

"For lunch."

"I don't care."

I could feel Luke and Caroline exchanging glances, but I hardly noticed. I was still staring at the stairwell where my mother had disappeared.

My mother.

I haven't seen her in almost a decade.

And now she was here.

Here to see me?

Or here to watch Rick sentenced to prison?

Or here for *him*?

I tried to push that idea out of my mind and focus on the other options. But if she was here to see me, wouldn't she have asked Mr. Raleigh where I was?

Maybe she was too shy. Or maybe she didn't even know I was going to be here. Maybe she was sorry for what she did last time. Maybe she's felt badly about it for all these years, and she came to see Rick finally get convicted.

I didn't know. Honestly, I didn't know her anymore. Maybe I never did.

Because when the police came to question her, she lied. She said that I never told her about the abuse, and that she had no reason to suspect that anything was wrong. It was one of the reasons the district attorney hadn't pursued my case. There was no corroborating evidence.

I was distracted all through lunch, but no one seemed surprised.

When we got back to the courthouse, I looked into the empty courtroom and then turned to stare at the top of the stairs, waiting. It was about ten minutes later when my mother came into view. She walked into the ladies' room.

My heart was beating so hard I was shaking. But my voice was almost steady when I said, "I'm going to go to the bathroom."

"I'll come with you," Caroline said.

"No. I'm fine." I didn't know what I was going to do, just that I needed to do it myself.

When I opened the door, there were two women talking while they touched up their makeup. I went to a free sink at the end of the line and washed my hands. A toilet flushed, my mother walked across the bathroom and turned on the water at one of the sinks further down the line. The talkers left. It was just the two of us now.

For a decade I've wanted to see her, and now there she was, mere feet from me, and I didn't have any idea what to say.

My mother finished washing her hands and started walking toward the door. I was watching her in the mirror, and I saw the moment when she noticed me. She stared at me for seconds, before finally taking a step closer, her face stunned.

"Alyson?"

I turned to face her.

She was there, right in front of me. But I couldn't form words.

There were tears in her eyes. "I have been so worried about you. Those people who took you from us wouldn't tell me where you were. Even after they dropped the charges against Rick, they wouldn't let you come home."

My mother reached toward me, but stopped, her hand hovering in the air. I looked at that hand, at the perfectly manicured nails and the rings on her finger, a massive diamond and a wedding band.

She married Rick.

Even after she knew.

She *married* him.

She came closer. We were so close we could have held hands the way we used to when I was small.

Mama looked at me with compassionate eyes. "Rick doesn't blame you for what you said. Neither of us do. We know the police pressured you into saying it was him."

And finally, I found my voice. "It was Rick."

Mama shook her head. "No, Baby. One of the men from the poker game hurt you. Rick was so upset. He couldn't get over the fact that one of his friends would do that to you."

"They didn't. Rick did."

"You don't remember," Mama said.

"I remember. I remember telling you he was hurting me."

"No." She spoke as if that one word could negate everything that had happened.

"I told you in the kitchen." My voice was rising. "And you called me a liar. You dragged me into the bathroom and washed my mouth out with soap while the eggs burned."

All of the gentle concern slid out of my mother's face. "That never happened," she snapped.

"I could barely walk when he was done with me, and you said nothing."

"Enough," my mother hissed at me. "You have to stop lying."

"I did," I said.

But she wasn't listening. "Do you realize how much trouble you caused us? Rick almost lost his job over the last investigation. And now this. Catalina never would have gotten the idea if you hadn't lied. Now she has her daughter spouting off all the same lies. Just so they can sue us later."

I knew Catalina. She was Rick's housekeeper when I lived there. She didn't have any children then. That makes the girl young. Less than ten.

I felt sick again.

And angry. So incredibly angry.

"What did the little girl say?" I asked my mother. "Did she say that Rick had her sit in his lap so he could touch her? Did he talk her into giving him 'presents'?"

The color was draining out of my mother's face. She took a step back. But I wasn't letting go.

"I never told Catalina any of that. The only way she would have known was if her daughter told her. Because Rick did the same things to her."

My mother was shaking her head. "You're lying."

"Why?" I was moving toward her now. "Why would I lie about this? Admitting that Rick was abusing me meant

I lost everything. Why would I do that if it wasn't true?"

"It-it was the police," Mama said. "They pressured you."

"No. That's Rick's lie."

"Rick is a good man," my mother said. But her voice was losing its conviction.

Mine was just angry. "Rick is a monster that you've been protecting when you should have been protecting that little girl. When you should have been protecting *me*."

There were tears on my cheeks and sobs catching in my throat. "Because we were worth protecting. We still are."

My mother faltered. I turned and walked out of the room.

It was time for me to testify.

Dear Olivia,

For the past two months I have been terrified of this day, of walking into that court room and facing that man. But I saw my mother today. And after I left her, I could barely feel my fear. It had been drowned out by pain and rage.

When I reached the hallway, I saw Mr. Raleigh waiting for me. Luke's parents both looked concerned. But it was Luke and Caroline who came to meet me in the middle of the hall. For a second, it was just the three of us.

They didn't say a word. They didn't have to. We would handle this the way we handle everything else. What ever happened, we were in this together.

When I started toward the doors, Luke and Caroline fell into step on either side of me. And mingled in with the pain and rage, I felt a sudden surge of love. Because I wasn't alone. My mother might have failed me, but I am still loved. Loved with a fierceness that makes me brave and a power that reminds me that I'm strong, strong enough to tell the truth. I already had. I had already told this story in all of its horrible pieces. And I had survived it. I had become better for it.

Over these last two months, I've realized that what happened with Rick wasn't my fault. You helped me with that. Because I know that there is nothing you could have done to deserve what Rick did to you. And realizing that helped me to be a little gentler with myself. We were victims of a monster who knew exactly how to lure us into loving him, trusting him. And then once the hook was set, he didn't just betray that trust, he made sure that we blamed ourselves for what happened. He set us up.

I still didn't know your real name. But I knew I was going to fight for you.

Because you are worth fighting for.

I felt power surging through me. The power of an avenging angel who had finally been set loose. I was ready to inflict justice. Not with a sword or fire, but with something far more dangerous. The truth.

Luke and Caroline opened the doors for me, and I walked into that courtroom with enough force to make every head turn. When Rick looked at me, I saw it. A flash of fear. In another second, it was gone, covered up by his usual calm expression. But I knew. He had seen the change in me.

I'm not a terrified little girl anymore.

I don't believe his lies.

I won't be defined by his disease.

Richard Wallace has lost his power over me.

And without his control containing me, I've

become a force to be reckoned with.

Rick was right to be afraid.

Because everything he did in secret was about to come into the light.

-Aly

SATURDAY, AUGUST 6

Tonight, for the first time in more than a century, every one of the Ballentine's windows was full of light. The north wing is complete, marking the end of the construction. So tonight, Mrs. Reese threw a cocktail party to celebrate the opening of the new wing and the end of the renovations. Hundreds of people came, including all of the kids from Group.

The entire north wing was open, but most of the guests ended up in the mural room. They were delighted by the work Mrs. Reese had commissioned. I couldn't stop looking at the wall she had conceded.

I finished the mural room three days after Judge Baxter found Richard Wallace guilty of seventeen separate assaults against Catalina's daughter. I know why the girl wasn't in the courtroom. And I'm glad she wasn't there for the testimony. But I wish she could have heard the judge sentence Rick to sixty years without parole for his "monstrous crimes." Just like I wish she could see the finished mural—especially the little girl who survived the fire.

A year ago, I would have said that surviving was enough. But not anymore. I've realized there is a world of difference between survival and restoration.

I wanted to see that little girl restored.

Putting her back together was the most difficult artistic task I have ever attempted. Mrs. Reese was right. It would have been easier to tear out the wall and start again. But the things that matter are rarely easy. And she was worth the time and the effort.

"She's beautiful," Luke said, sliding an arm around me.

"She looks like she's about to step out of the wall and dance," Caroline said. "Which would be fantastic, by the way."

"I hope she does," I said.

After so many years trapped in a blackened tomb, it's time for her to come alive again.

Dear _____,

I don't know your name. But I know a few things about you. I know that you've felt isolated in your heartache and burdened by your secrets. I know that you sometimes wonder if you're too broken to ever be genuinely loved.

This is by far the hardest story I've ever written. And there were so many days when I wanted to give up and write something easy. But I didn't. Because of you.

You needed to be reminded that you are strong, and you are brave. And no matter how dark these last few chapters of your life have been, your story isn't finished. It's just beginning.

I hope that you'll write your name on the space I left for you on the dedication page. Because I wrote this book for you.

-Heather

If you enjoyed this book, and have two or three minutes, would you write a review on Amazon or Goodreads? I would greatly appreciate it! And be sure to visit me at www.heathermullaly.com.

ACKNOWLEDGEMENTS

Mom and Dad, thank you for being the amazing people that you are, for loving me, believing in me, and teaching me to pursue dreams with tenacity.

Chris, thank you for calling me an author long before I was willing to use the term. Words have power, and yours helped me to see past my doubts.

Tom, my love, my best friend, and biggest supporter in all things, thank you for your unwavering love and encouragement.

Hannah, Elizabeth, and Julia, thank you for putting up with those moments when Mom was lost in the realm of writing.

Meg Whelpley, Allison Yoder, and Erin Chinn, my fearless beta readers, thank you for your thoughts, your time, and your willingness to walk with me along this long journey. Your friendship is priceless to me.

Sarah Aronson and my friends at The Highlights Foundation, thank you for believing in this story before I did.

Sara Preston, Rebecca Aronson, and Stephanie Cohen thank you for applying your editing prowess to Aly's story. You each helped this book to become a better version of itself.

Isaiah 61:1

ABOUT THE AUTHOR

Heather Mullaly is a passionate believer in the power of story. When she isn't writing them, reading them, or listening to them, she can usually be found baking something that involves chocolate, thinking up new story ideas before she's finished the two she's currently writing, or hanging out with her family, who happen to be even more fantastic than the characters in her head.

Made in the USA
Middletown, DE
08 September 2021